John
Grisham
THEODORE
BOONE
The Scandal

HODDER

First published in Great Britain in 2016 by Hodder & Stoughton
An Hachette UK company

First published in paperback in 2017

2

Copyright © Boone & Boone, LLC 2016

The right of John Grisham to be identified as the Author
of the Work has been asserted by him in accordance with
the Copyright, Designs and Patents Act 1988.

A CIP catalogue record for this title is available from the British Library

Paperback ISBN 978 1 444 76773 5

Printed and bound by Clays Ltd, Elcograf S.p.A.

Hodder & Stoughton policy is to use papers that are natural, renewable
and recyclable products and made from wood grown in sustainable
forests. The logging and manufacturing processes are expected to
conform to the environmental regulations of the country of origin.

Hodder & Stoughton Ltd
Carmelite House
50 Victoria Embankment
London EC4Y 0DZ

www.hodder.co.uk

THEODORE
BOONE
The Scandal

Also by John Grisham

THEODORE
BOONE
The Scandal

Theodore Boone woke up in a foul mood. In fact, he'd gone to bed in a foul mood, and things had not improved during the night. As a few rays of morning sun lit his room, he stared at the ceiling and tried to think of ways to avoid this entire week. Generally, he enjoyed school—his friends, the teachers, most of the classes, debating—but there were times when he just wanted to stay in bed. This was one of those times, the worst week of the year. Beginning tomorrow, Tuesday, and running through Friday, he and every other eighth grader would be stuck at their desks taking a series of dreadful tests.

Judge knew something was wrong, and at some point had left his spot beside Theo's bed and assumed his spot on top of the covers. Mrs. Boone frowned on the idea of the dog sleeping in Theo's bed, but she was downstairs having her quiet time with the morning newspaper and wouldn't know. Or would she? Occasionally she noticed dog hair on the covers and asked Theo if Judge was sleeping with him. Most of the time Theo said yes, but quickly followed the admission with the question: "What am I supposed to do?" He couldn't watch the dog while he, Theo, was sound asleep. And, to be honest, Theo didn't really want the dog in the bed with him. Judge had the irritating habit of stretching himself out smack in the middle of things and expecting Theo to retreat to the edges, where he often came within inches of crashing to the floor and waking up with a sore head. No, Theo preferred that Judge sleep on his little doggy bed down below.

The truth was, Judge did whatever he wanted to do, and not only in Theo's room but in every room in the house.

On days like today, Theo envied his dog. What a life: no school, no homework, no tests, no pressure. He ate whenever he wanted, napped most of the day at the office, and seemed unconcerned about most things. The Boones took care of his needs, and he did anything he wanted.

Reluctantly, Theo got out of bed, rubbed his dog's head, said good morning, but not with as much enthusiasm as usual, and went to the bathroom. Last week the orthodontist had readjusted his braces, and his jaws still ached. He grinned at himself in the mirror, took stock of the mouthful of metal that he despised, and tried to find hope in the fact that he *might* get the braces off just in time to start the ninth grade.

He stepped into the shower and thought about the ninth grade. High school. He just wasn't ready for it. He was thirteen and quite content at Strattenburg Middle School, where he liked his teachers, most of them anyway, and was captain of the Debate Team, almost an Eagle Scout and, well, thought of himself as a leader. He was certainly the only kid lawyer in the school, the only kid he knew of who dreamed of being either a big-time trial lawyer or a brilliant young judge. He couldn't make up his mind. In the ninth grade he would be just another lowly freshman at the bottom of the pile. Freshmen got no respect in high school. Middle school was okay because Theo had found his place, a place that would disappear in a few months. High school was all about football, basketball, cheerleaders, driving, dating, band, theatre, large classes, clothes, shaving, and, well, growing up. He just wasn't ready for it. Most of his friends wanted to hurry along and grow up, but not Theo.

He stepped out of the shower and dried off. Judge was watching him and thinking about nothing but breakfast. Such a lucky dog.

As Theo brushed his teeth, or rather cleaned his braces, he admitted that life was changing. High school was slowly rising on the horizon. One of its most important and unpleasant warning signs was standardized testing, a horrible idea cooked up by some experts far away. Those people had decided that it was important to give the same tests at the same time to every eighth grader in the state so that the folks in charge of Strattenburg Middle School and all the other schools would know how they stacked up. That was one reason for the tests. Another reason, at least in Strattenburg, was to separate the eighth graders into three groups for high school. The smartest would be fast-tracked into an Honors program. The weaker students would be placed on a slower track, one without an official name because there was no suitable name for the "slow track." And the average kids would be treated normally and allowed to enjoy high school without special treatment.

Yet another reason for the tests was to measure how well the teachers were doing. If a teacher's class did really well, he or she would qualify for a bonus. And if the class did poorly, all kinds of bad things might happen to the teacher. He or she might even be fired.

Needless to say, the entire process of testing, scoring, tracking, and evaluating teachers had become hotly controversial. The students, of course, hated it. Most of the teachers didn't like it. Almost all parents wanted their kids in the Honors classes, and almost all were disappointed. Those with kids on the "slow track" were mad, even embarrassed.

And so the debate raged. Mrs. Boone was firmly opposed to the testing, so, of course, Mr. Boone supported it. The family had talked about testing for weeks, over dinner and in the car, and even while watching television. For a month, the eighth-grade teachers had been preparing the students for the tests. "Teaching to the tests," was the favorite description, which meant no creative teaching was being done and no one was having fun in class.

Theo was already sick of the tests, and they had not even started.

He dressed, grabbed his backpack, and went downstairs, Judge at his heels. He said hello to his mother, who, as always, was curled up on the sofa in her robe, sipping coffee and reading the newspaper. Mr. Boone always left early and joined his friends for coffee and gossip at the same downtown diner.

Theo fixed two bowls of Cheerios and put one on the floor for Judge. They almost always ate in silence, but occasionally Mrs. Boone joined them for a chat. She did this when she suspected something was bothering Theo. Today, she entered the kitchen, poured more coffee, and took a seat across from her son. "What's up today?" she asked.

"More reviewing, more practicing how to take the tests."

"Are you nervous?"

"Not really. I'm just tired already. I don't do well on these tests, so I don't like them."

It was true. Theo was almost a straight-A student, with an occasional B in the sciences, but he had never done well on standardized tests. "What if I don't make the Honors track next year?" he asked.

"Teddy, you're going to excel in high school, college, and law school, if you choose to go there. Don't worry about where they put you in the ninth grade."

"Thanks, Mom." Her words felt good in spite of the fact that she called him "Teddy," a little nickname that, thankfully, only she used, and only when they were alone.

Theo had friends whose parents were turning flips and losing sleep over the tests. If their kids didn't make Honors, the parents were convinced their kids were headed for miserable lives. The whole thing seemed silly to Theo.

She said, "I suppose you know that there is a backlash across the country against these tests. They are becoming very unpopular, and there appears to be widespread cheating."

"How do you cheat on a standardized test?"

"I'm not sure, but I've read about some of the cheating. In one district the teachers changed answers. Hard to believe, isn't it?"

"Why would a teacher do that?"

"Well, in that case, the school was not very good and on probation with the district. Plus, the teachers wanted to qualify for a bonus. None of it makes any sense."

"I think I'm getting sick. Do I look pale?"

"No, Teddy. You look perfectly healthy."

It was eight o'clock, time to move. Theo rinsed both bowls and left them in the sink, same as always. He kissed his mom on the cheek and said, "I'm off."

"Do you have lunch money?" she asked, the same question five days a week.

"Always."

"And your homework is complete?"

"It's perfect, Mom."

"And I'll see you when?"

"I'll stop by the office after school." Theo stopped by the office every day after school, without fail, but Mrs. Boone always asked.

"Be careful," she said. "And remember to smile."

"I'm smiling, Mom."

"Love you, Teddy."

"Love you back."

Theo stepped outside and said good-bye to Judge, who would ride in the car with Mrs. Boone to the office where he would spend his day sleeping and eating and worrying about nothing. Theo jumped on his bike and sped away, once again wishing he could be a dog for the next four days.

2

At 8:40 the bell rang and Mr. Mount called his troops to order. Usually, on Mondays, they were fairly rowdy and gabbing nonstop over whatever happened during the weekend. Today, though, they were more subdued. The truth was that everyone in the eighth grade, from the kids to the teachers to the administrators, maybe even the secretaries and janitors, was dreading the week to come.

Woody raised his hand and said, "Say, Mr. Mount, I have an idea. Since I don't want to be on the Honors track, and since I'm far too smart for the slow track, why can't I just take a pass and be normal and skip all these tests?"

Mr. Mount smiled and said, "Because the school says

you have to take the tests. It's one way of making sure our school is doing well."

"Our school is in the top ten percent in the state, or at least that's what we're told all the time around here," Woody replied. "Of course we're doing well. We have great teachers, brilliant students, the works."

"Sorry. Look, guys, I'm not crazy about these tests myself, but I'm not making the rules."

Woody was on a roll. "Okay, but just look around the room. We know that Chase and Joey and Aaron and maybe Theo will score high and make Honors. We also know that the slow ones—Justin and Darren and, of course, Edward— will end up in the slow group. Why can't the rest of us just admit that we're normal and skip the tests?"

Amid the hissing, Edward said, "Speak for yourself, you idiot."

"My IQ is much higher than yours," Darren shot from across the room.

"You almost flunked phys ed," Justin yelled from the back.

"Okay, okay," Mr. Mount said, holding up both hands. "That's enough for now."

"I think I'm going to puke," Woody said. "I'm really getting sick."

"Knock it off. First period will be with Ms. Garman to review math. Next will be language arts with Ms. Eberlee, then a fifteen-minute break. I know you guys are excited. Let's go."

They moaned and groaned and trudged out of the room, as if headed for a firing squad.

After three hours of torture, the students were especially happy to gather in the cafeteria for a thirty-minute lunch break. Theo wanted to get away from the boys and happened to see April Finnemore sitting alone. He took his tray of spaghetti and salad and eased into the chair next to her. "Having any fun?" he asked.

"Hello, Theo," she said quietly. They were close friends, nothing romantic or anything like that, though Woody and the others often teased Theo about his weird girlfriend. April was different, not weird. She was serious, often moody, and often misunderstood by her classmates. She dressed more like a boy than a girl, wore her hair very short, and had no interest in fashion and teen gossip and social media and all the other stuff she deemed trivial. She loved art and wanted to be a painter, in Paris or Santa Fe, somewhere far from home because home was not a happy place. Her parents were nuts. Her older brother and sister had already fled. She was often alone and left to fend for herself.

Theo was about the only kid in the eighth grade who tried to understand her. "Are you as bored as I am?" he asked.

"Totally. I can't wait until Friday afternoon and these tests are behind us."

"Are you nervous?" he asked as he shoveled in a load of spaghetti.

"Yes, very. I have to make the Honors track, Theo, because it offers more art programs. I don't care about anything else. The art classes are small, and the best teachers are in Honors." She spoke softly as she pushed some salad around her plate. She had the appetite of a bird. She hadn't touched her roll, and Theo had his eye on it.

"You'll do fine, April. You could make straight A's if you wanted to." She didn't, because neither parent pushed her at home. She was absent more than any other student, and when she was in class she was often unprepared. She made perfect grades in French and Spanish but was uninterested in everything else. Except art.

"How are things at home?" he asked, glancing around. It was a loaded question because the answer could be anything. The Finnemores lived in a rental house in a lesser part of town, and April kept her other friends away from the house. But Theo understood.

"Okay, I guess. About the same. I just stay in my room, do art, and read books."

"I'm glad things are okay."

"Thanks, Theo. You're going to do fine on the tests."

"I don't really care."

"Yes, you do. You're a good student and you're competitive. You want to be at the top of every class, including law school. Don't tell me you don't care."

"Okay, maybe a little. But law school seems like a long way off."

"It is. Let's get through high school first."

"Deal."

A boy named Pete approached them from the other side of the cafeteria and looked as if he wanted to say something. He was an eighth grader from another section, a kid Theo hardly knew. His hands were empty; he had no lunch tray, no brown bag. Slowly, he sat down and glanced nervously at April, then at Theo. "Hi, Pete," Theo said.

"Can I talk to you?" he said timidly, as if April had suddenly vanished.

"Uh, sure. What's up?"

"Can we talk, just the two of us?"

"Just finishing up here," April said as she grabbed her tray and stood. "See you later, Theo."

"Sorry," Pete said after she was gone. "I didn't mean to interrupt."

Well, you sure did a fine job of it, Theo thought, but said nothing. The kid had a bruise on his cheek and looked frightened. "Can we go outside?" he asked.

"Have you eaten?" Theo asked.

He nodded slightly, as if he wasn't sure. "Yes."

Theo stuffed his mouth with as much spaghetti as possible and took his tray to the counter. They stepped outside onto the playground and walked around the edge, far from the other kids. They walked and walked and Pete seemed unable to speak, so Theo finally broke the ice with, "What happened to your cheek?"

"You know all about lawyers and stuff, right?"

"I guess. Both of my parents are lawyers. I've sort of absorbed a lot. What's going on?"

"My dad drinks a lot, does some drugs. He came home late Saturday night drunk, and he and my mom got into a big fight. He smacked her around, busted a lip, there was some blood. I'm the oldest kid, two younger sisters, and I tried to help my mom. He slapped me a few times. My sister Sharon, she's ten, called 911 and the police came.

They arrested my dad and took him away. It was terrible, just terrible. He's in jail, and now my mom, and me and my sisters, too, are really afraid of what will happen when he gets out."

Theo listened carefully as they continued walking. "Has this happened before?"

"Yes, but he's never hit me. A few months back, my mom threatened to call the police and he settled down. He said he would kill her if she ever told anyone. But if she tells the police now, then he'll just go to jail and lose his job. We don't have much money, Theo. My mom works two part-time jobs, and, well, I guess we're just in big trouble. What's my mom supposed to do? Keep it quiet and keep getting beat up until he kills her, or tell the police everything and put him away in jail? We don't know what to do, Theo."

Theo was only thirteen. These questions would stump any adult. "He's still in jail?"

"Yes. He called the house last night from jail and said he would get out today. My mom is scared to death. So am I."

"Does your mom know a lawyer?"

Pete grunted. What a ridiculous question. "We can't afford a lawyer, Theo. That's why I'm talking to you."

"I'm not a lawyer, and I can't give legal advice."

"I know that. But what should we do?"

Theo wasn't sure what to do, but he had to do something. If he did nothing, Pete's mother and maybe Pete himself could be in real danger. Theo said, "My mother will know what to do. She's the best divorce lawyer in town, and she's not afraid of anything. Can you and your mom come to our office this afternoon?"

"I don't know. I'm not sure my mom will do that because if my dad finds out she's talking to a lawyer he might go crazy again. She's trapped, Theo. My mom is trapped and doesn't know where to go or what to do."

Theo stopped and put a hand on Pete's shoulder. "Here's the deal, Pete. I'm not sure what to do and you're not sure what to do, but we're just kids, right? My mother deals with this stuff all the time, and she'll give your mom the best advice possible. She will know exactly what to do. Trust me, and trust her. I'll give you the address of our office, and I'll talk to my mother. I'll meet you there this afternoon, and things will start to get better. I promise."

Pete's lip quivered and his eyes were moist. "Thanks, Theo," he managed to say before his voice choked up.

An hour later, Theo was suffering through a review of basic biology when his mind drifted back to his conversation with

Pete. The poor kid was living a nightmare, afraid of getting punched by his brute of a father and afraid for his mother's life. How was a kid like Pete supposed to sit through four days of testing, concentrate on the exams, and score well enough to get properly placed on the right track for high ochool? And that placement could well determine his future. It made little sense, at least to Theo.

3

When the last bell rang, Theo grabbed his backpack and fled the school. He jumped on his bike and raced away. Ten minutes later he slid to a stop in front of Boone & Boone, a two-story office in what was once a family residence on Park Street. He pushed his bike up the front sidewalk and parked it on the porch. He took a deep breath and walked inside, where he was immediately assaulted by Elsa, the law firm's ancient secretary and receptionist. She also considered herself to be Theo's second mother. When she saw him she gushed, "Well, hello, Theo!" and jumped from her chair to grab him. She hugged him tightly, then pushed back, looked at his attire, and said, "Didn't you wear that shirt last Friday?"

"I did not." He found it so irritating to be examined daily

by Elsa. He was thirteen; he didn't care what he wore. Why should she?

"How was your day?" she said, pinching a cheek.

"Awful. Just awful. And it only gets worse tomorrow."

"Now, Theo, just think of all the unlucky kids around the world who don't have nice schools and good teachers and healthy lunches. You should always count your blessings and—"

"I know, I know," Theo said, stepping back. He got so tired of these little lectures. "What's in the kitchen?" He was always starving by three o'clock in the afternoon, and there was always something to snack on in the firm's kitchen. Judge finally got up from his bed under Elsa's desk, one of his many resting places throughout the offices, and walked over to say hello. Theo rubbed his head. What a life.

"I think Dorothy brought some brownies," Elsa said.

"Not those little peanut butter things. They taste like cardboard." Not even Judge would touch Dorothy's brownies.

"Now, Theo," Elsa said, already losing interest and eager to get back to work. Elsa was skinny and had no appetite, and she liked to show off her thinness by wearing all manner of tight pants and sweaters. Mrs. Boone said that Elsa wore things that only she could get by with because she was at least seventy years old.

"Is my mother in?" he asked.

"Yes, but she's with a client."

"I need to book an appointment with her."

"Theo, you don't have to make an appointment to see your mother."

"It's not for me, Elsa, but for a friend. I'm not getting a divorce yet."

Elsa glanced at a large calendar in the center of her desk. It was her daily planner, a terribly important sheet of paper because it kept track of everything from meetings with clients and court appointments to vacations and Theo's visits to the orthodontist. "She's free at four thirty."

"Thanks," Theo said. "If a guy named Pete Holland calls, let me talk to him."

Theo bounded up the stairs to the second floor, the domain of his father. As usual, Mr. Boone was sitting behind his large cluttered desk, pipe in his mouth, tie pulled loose, with the look of a man who'd been plowing through paperwork for days. He smiled and said, "Hello, Theo, a good day at school?"

Theo fell into a chair and Judge sat beside him. "Just awful, Dad, terrible. I'm sick of school."

"Well, dropping out is not an option. I suggest you stop the whining and get tough. These tests are important, and you need to do well."

Thanks for nothing, Dad. They talked for a few minutes

until the phone rang. Mr. Boone reached for it and said, "Now shove off and go do your homework."

Perhaps the only good thing about the week was that there would be no homework. Theo went downstairs, rummaged through the refrigerator, found nothing but some stale doughnuts, and eventually wandered back to his small office where he killed some time. Bored, he was soon sleepy, so he put his feet on his desk, kicked back in his chair, and was about to doze off when his mother tapped on his door and stepped in.

"Hello, Theo. Elsa said you needed to see me."

"Sure, Mom. There's a kid at school who needs your help."

"What's the problem?"

"It's a long story, but the kid and his mother might be in danger."

"Let's go to my office and talk."

It was almost five p.m. when Pete Holland arrived with his mother and two younger sisters. The little girls were wide-eyed and seemed too frightened to speak. Pete, at thirteen, was trying to be the man of the family, but he, too, was overwhelmed. His mother, Carrie, had a swollen eye and a cut on her upper lip. She looked like she had been crying for hours and began again as soon as Mrs. Boone introduced herself and said she could help. She led Carrie into her office and closed the door. Theo pointed to the conference room and said, "Let's wait in there." Pete and his sisters followed Theo while Elsa hurried to the kitchen. She returned with the same stale doughnuts and some soft drinks. Even Judge seemed concerned and allowed the girls to rub his head.

Pete said, "My dad got out of jail this afternoon and he's looking for us. My mom's really scared and doesn't know what to do."

Sharon, the ten-year-old, finally spoke and said, "Mom says we can't go home." Sally, the seven-year-old, chewed on a doughnut and looked at Theo as if he had two heads.

"What are we going to do?" Sharon asked, as if Theo had all the answers.

Elsa, who had been through similar dramas, said, "Mrs. Boone will know what to do. Right now, let's just have a chat and talk about school. Did you bring your backpacks? Maybe we could do some homework." They shook their heads. No backpacks.

Since it was Monday, Theo called his uncle Ike and said he couldn't make their usual Monday meeting. He promised to stop by later in the week.

Mr. Boone stopped by to say good-bye and quickly realized that perhaps he should hang around for a while. He took off his coat, sat at the table, and began convincing Sally that she should chat with him. In spite of the law firm's efforts to comfort the children, the mood was still awkward, even tense. Their mother was talking to a lawyer, and their lives were unsettled.

After an hour, the door to Mrs. Boone's office opened. She and Mrs. Holland walked out and entered the conference room. Mr. Boone introduced himself properly; Mrs. Holland was too upset to say much. Her eyes were wet, and she dabbed them with a tissue. Mrs. Boone looked at Elsa and Mr. Boone and said, "Mr. Holland posted bond this afternoon and was released from jail around two. He's charged with assault and has a court date next week. He's been calling Mrs. Holland nonstop and leaving some messages that are threatening. It appears as though he's driving around town, searching for his family."

Mrs. Holland interrupted with, "And he's drinking, I can tell."

Mrs. Boone nodded and continued, "I've talked to the police, and they are looking for him. I have advised Mrs. Holland not to go home tonight and she agrees. There is a friend or two the family could possibly stay with, but her husband would probably find them. I've called the shelter and there's no available space, at least not for tonight."

"So we have to hide?" Pete asked.

"We're hiding now," his mother said.

"I just want to go home," Sharon said, and began crying.

"We can't go home," Pete said sharply.

"What's the plan?" Mr. Boone asked.

"I think we should go to our house and have a pizza party," Mrs. Boone replied. "We'll watch television and see what happens."

"Great idea," Mr. Boone said.

"I'll get the pizza," Elsa said, jumping to her feet.

Sally looked at Mr. Boone and managed to smile.

Two hours later, the Boones' den was covered with quilts, pillows, and kids. The pizza was long gone. Sally huddled with her mother on the sofa while Pete, Sharon, Theo, Elsa, and Judge were sprawled about the floor, all watching reruns of *Everybody Loves Raymond*. Mr. Boone was in his study reading a book, and Mrs. Boone eased from room to room, occasionally talking quietly on the phone in the kitchen. Theo met her there and whispered, "What's going on, Mom?"

She whispered back, "The police have not been able to find Mr. Holland. They can't go home tonight; it's just too dangerous. He's probably drinking, probably drunk by now, and who knows what will happen. They'll have to stay here tonight."

Theo understood and didn't mind protecting the family. "But what about tomorrow?"

"Mrs. Holland's parents live about four hours from here. That might be an option, maybe for a few days. The police will eventually find Mr. Holland and arrest him again for making threats. I'll probably go to court and ask the judge for a protective order. As of now, she says she wants to file for a divorce and get him out of the house, but that might not be so easy. I don't know, Theo, we'll just have to wait and see. Things could change by the hour. The important thing is to keep them safe."

"She's crazy if she doesn't get a divorce."

"It's never that easy, Theo, believe me. A lot of women put up with abuse because they think they have to. They can't afford to live without their husband and his job. I see this all the time."

"I'm not going to be a divorce lawyer."

"Let's talk about that later, okay?"

"Sure, Mom, and thanks for doing this. I feel like I'm responsible."

"You did the right thing, Theo. Lawyers have to get in-volved in unpleasant cases to help people. Who else could help at this point?"

"The police."

"And they're trying. You guys can sleep in the den and watch TV until late. Let's try and make it fun."

"Does this mean I can skip school tomorrow?"

"It does not."

When Judge began growling at 2:14 a.m., he was standing near Theo's head and staring at the front door less than twenty feet away. Theo woke up and knew something was wrong. He crawled to a window and saw a pickup truck parked at the curb by the mailbox. Then he saw a shadow move near the front steps.

"What is it, Theo?" Mrs. Holland whispered. She was on the sofa, wrapped up in a quilt with Sally. It was no surprise she had not been sleeping.

"Someone's out there," Theo said. He scampered to the foyer and turned on the outside lights. A split second later, a loud boom rattled the front door, again and again. A very angry man was yelling and banging with his fists. Judge began barking loudly as everybody in the house panicked and bolted upright. Mr. Boone yelled, "Call the police!" and Mrs. Boone went for the phone.

"Open up!" the man yelled as he banged away. "I know you're in there, Carrie!"

"It's Randy," Mrs. Holland said. "Good old Randy. Drunk as a skunk."

"Take the kids to the kitchen," Mr. Boone said. He walked to the door and said, "We're calling the police, Mr. Holland."

"Open the door! I have the right to see my wife and kids."

"They don't want to see you right now. Please stop banging or you'll wake up the neighbors."

"Don't really care. I want my family!"

"Why don't you leave, and we'll sit down tomorrow and discuss everything? There's nothing to be gained by causing a big scene in the middle of the night."

Judge was barking like an idiot but not advancing on the door. Mr. Boone growled, "Shut up, Judge. Theo, get the dog!"

"The police are right around the corner," Mrs. Boone said softly as she stepped in from the kitchen. "Keep talking to him."

Mr. Boone cracked the door but left the chain hooked. He looked at Randy through the glass of a metal storm door. When Randy saw the crack, he began banging away again. "Open the door! I want my wife and kids!"

"Please settle down, Mr. Holland," Mr. Boone said. From across the street, the lights of the Ferguson home came on. Suddenly, Randy picked up a large rock from the flower bed and crashed it through the glass of the storm door. Mr. Boone managed to slam the wooden door just as everything shattered. Judge bravely retreated to a safe spot behind the sofa, whimpering. In the kitchen, Sally and Sharon were crying as Pete tried to console them.

"He's crazy," Mr. Boone said in shock.

"I told you so," Carrie said from the kitchen doorway. "Crazy and drunk."

"What a cheap door!" Randy yelled, and he began laughing. Theo was hiding behind a chair and peeking through the blinds. The man was indeed frightening. He was thick and burly, with a beard, and long hair sticking out from under a cap. He was weaving and staggering, obviously intoxicated. He took a step back and bellowed, "You think you're so smart, don't you, Carrie? Well, you're pretty stupid. I found you by tracking your cell phone. Pretty stupid." He almost fell off the stoop but caught himself on an iron railing.

Mr. Boone cracked the door about an inch and calmly

said, "Mr. Holland, I've called the police and they are on the way. Now would you please settle down?"

"I don't care who you call," he yelled. "Call the cops, call the sheriff, call the FBI, hell, call the Marines for all I care. I just want to see my family."

Calmly, Mr. Boone said, "Well, they don't want to see you, and you're headed back to jail if you don't leave."

"I ain't leaving, okay, mister? Not without my wife and kids. You have no right to keep them in there."

More lights from across the street. Mr. and Mrs. Ferguson were standing on the front porch in their pajamas. Randy tried to pick up another rock from the flower bed but lost his balance and fell into some shrubs. As he scrambled to get up, mumbling and cursing and wiping off dirt, he noticed the Fergusons watching him. This upset him, so he yelled, "Why don't you folks just mind your own business?"

The Fergusons said nothing.

Randy pointed at them and yelled, "Bunch of nosy people in this neighborhood, that's what I think. I might just come over there and throw a rock through your door. How would you like that?" But as he walked across the Boones' front lawn, he lost his balance again, then tripped over his own feet. Down he went, tumbling and clawing to get up.

Thankfully, blue lights appeared at the end of the street.

Randy Holland surrendered without a fight, and when the policemen slapped on the handcuffs and led him to the patrol car, his family was watching from the front window, and all four were in tears.

With her husband back in jail, Mrs. Holland decided to return home and put the kids to bed. She thanked the Boones repeatedly, as did Pete and Sharon, and they left around 3:30. As Theo was helping his parents straighten up the den, he said, "Gosh, there's no way I can go to school tomorrow. I'm already exhausted."

To which his mother said sternly, "Then I suggest you get upstairs right now and go to sleep."

"And take your dog with you," Mr. Boone said. "What a great guard dog."

"But what about school?"

"You can sleep until seven thirty," Mrs. Boone said.

"Wow. Thanks. You guys are really sympathetic."

"Knock it off," Mr. Boone said. "I'm tired of the whining."

5

The mood in the auditorium was somber early Tuesday morning as the entire eighth grade filed in. Ten perfect rows of seventeen desks each covered the floor, with four odd ones along the back wall. Each homeroom adviser showed his or her students to their places. Mr. Mount's gang was in row two, and they sat in alphabetical order. Theo was third from the front, with Ricardo Alvarez and Edward Benton in front of him. To his right was a girl named Tess Carver; to his left was a girl whose first name was Lellie. He didn't know her last name. There were 174 in all, and Theo knew most of them, but it was impossible to know everyone, especially the girls. The school was in its third year of an experiment that separated the eighth-grade boys and girls.

Theo nodded at Pete, who was four rows over and half the way back. He wondered if Pete was as tired as he was. Probably so. What a night. He himself was still rattled by what had happened. He couldn't imagine the confused state of mind Pete was in.

The principal, Mrs. Gladwell, made a few opening remarks, boring standard stuff about trying to relax and trying to work efficiently. They would be on the clock, and it was important to finish each section, and so on. This had already been covered more than once. The tests would last for three hours, with only two short breaks, then lunch. They would then spend three hours each afternoon prepping for the next day's tests. Friday afternoon seemed like a year away.

The teachers passed out the exams as quickly as possible. Theo had a knot in his stomach as he took his. When every student had an exam, Mr. Mount, the head proctor for the day, told them to begin. As the students began, their teachers fanned out through the auditorium in a display of force. The message was clear: Keep your eyes on your own exam.

The room was silent. The agony had begun.

During the lunch break, Theo ate hurriedly and went to find Pete. They walked the same path as the day before, along the edge of the playground and away from anyone else. Pete said he couldn't go back to sleep after he got home, and he was too tired to think. He was blowing the exam and didn't care. His mother had talked to the police, and they had assured her Mr. Holland would remain in jail for a few days, so at least they would be safe. "What's a felony?" Pete asked.

"It's a more serious crime. Misdemeanors are small crimes. Felonies are not. Why?"

"The police said he's charged with a third-class felony called malicious destruction of property. I guess that means a lot of jail time, right?"

"Probably, but I doubt if he'll get a long prison sentence. Just a few weeks in the county jail. Who knows?"

A divorce, a jail sentence, the loss of a job; it was a lot for a kid to comprehend. "Thanks for last night, Theo."

"It was nothing."

"My mom is supposed to see your mom this afternoon, I guess to talk about the divorce. I can't believe this."

"My mom is very good at finding ways to avoid divorce, Pete. She almost always gets the couple to agree to meet with a marriage counselor. Don't give up yet."

"Thanks, Theo."

"And don't give up on these tests either."

"I'd like to run away right now."

Me too, Theo wanted to say, but instead he played tough

and said, "Can't do that, Pete. You gotta buckle down and concentrate."

"I'll try."

The final bell rang at 3:30, and Theo was on his bike within seconds and flying away from the school. At the office, he said a quick hello to Elsa, his mother, and Judge, and raced five blocks to the VFW building where Troop 1440 met on the first and third Tuesdays of each month. This was the second Tuesday and not an official meeting, but when the Major, their scoutmaster, called, you didn't ask questions.

Theo was a few months away from the big prize: Eagle Scout. He had twenty merit badges, including all but one of those required, and the Major was pushing him hard. He expected all of his Scouts to become Eagles. Theo suspected the Major wanted to review his progress, something he liked to do privately when the troop wasn't meeting. He parked his bike next to Woody's and went inside. The Major was chatting with Cal, Woody, Hardie, and Mason, an eighth grader from East Middle School.

The boys gathered around their scoutmaster in folding chairs, and he said, "I understand this is a rough week for eighth graders, all that testing they put you through."

"It's awful," Woody blurted.

Hardie said, "Four straight days of testing."

The Major smiled and said, "Well, I have an idea. This troop has thirty-nine Scouts as of today and sixteen of those are in the eighth grade. I know you're having a tough week so I have an idea for a little camping trip this weekend. It's completely voluntary."

The boys perked up. Nothing excited them like a weekend in the woods.

The Major continued: "There's a new hike that's been opened in the Sassaqua National Park, a forty-mile trail that requires two nights in the wild. You have to hike in with everything on your back—tent, sleeping bag, food, clothes, toilet paper. It has some tough spots, some cliffs and steep inclines, there's a gorge and some caves. It runs along the Sassaqua River, in the most secluded part of the park, and the scenery is said to be spectacular. The plan is to take off Friday afternoon as soon as the tests are over. It's about a two-hour drive, so we should get there well before dark. I think we can get five miles into the woods before we set up camp. Who's in?"

The boys were almost too stunned to speak. The troop spent one weekend each month in the woods, and those adventures were not to be missed. This, though, was something even better. A small group of the best Scouts hiking with the Major and living out of their backpacks. They were all in!

Theo was beyond thrilled. Whatever was planned for his weekend would simply get shoved aside. Then Cal dropped his head and said, "Shoot. My grandmother is coming this weekend, and there's no way I can leave town."

"Sorry," the Major said. "Woody, Hardie, and Theo—you guys call the other eighth graders and see who can go. We need to get this organized as quickly as possible."

"What about the rest of the troop?" Theo asked.

"Well, I'll promise the younger guys that this will become an annual hike, sort of a reward after the tests. For the older guys, I'll find some way to make it up. I don't foresee a problem."

"Who cares about the older guys?" Woody said. "Let's go."

"Get it planned," the Major ordered. "Use your checklists and don't forget anything. You'll be in the woods with no way out except on foot. Planning is crucial."

Theo was required by family tradition to stop by his uncle Ike's office every Monday afternoon for a visit. If Ike was in a good mood, the time was enjoyable. If Ike was in a bad mood, Theo didn't stay very long. There was about a fifty-fifty split in Ike's moods. He had once been a respected lawyer who specialized in tax matters. Now he kept the books for a few clients and didn't make much money. He had once worked from a nice office over at Boone & Boone. Now he worked in a dump above a Greek deli and had no secretary. He once was married and had two children. Now he was divorced and the kids, now adults and Theo's first cousins, never made it back to Strattenburg and had nothing to do with their father. According to Theo's mother, Ike had once been quite stylish, with dark suits and fine silk ties. Now he wore faded jeans, sandals, and T-shirts, and he kept his long gray hair pulled tightly in a ponytail. As Theo was learning, the old version of Ike was far different from the one he knew.

And that was fine. Theo adored his uncle Ike, and the feeling was mutual.

Since Theo had spent Monday afternoon with the Holland family, he decided to stop by Ike's on Tuesday after the quick and pleasant meeting with the Major. As always, Ike was at his desk, surrounded by piles of paperwork, with Bob Dylan playing softly on the stereo and a can of beer beside his phone. "Well, how's my favorite nephew?" he asked, the same question every time.

Theo often wondered how and why adults got in the habit of asking the same questions over and over, but he knew there was no clear explanation. "I'm doing lousy, and I'm your only nephew."

"Oh, that's right. A full week of testing for robots. What a stupid idea. Back when I was a kid, teachers were allowed to teach, but now ..." He held up his hands and said, "Sorry, I think we had this discussion last week."

"We did. A drunk guy tried to break in our house last night," Theo said with a smile. Before each visit he always tried to think of something interesting to tell Ike.

"Well, do tell," Ike said as he sipped his beer.

With great enthusiasm, Theo told the story of the Holland family and Mr. Holland's near-assault on the Boone household. He managed to make the event somewhat more frightening than it had really been, but he knew Ike appreciated a good story. Ike himself had said that he'd never heard a story he couldn't improve with a little exaggeration.

Theo went on, "And Mom says they'll keep him in jail for a few days and charge him with a felony."

"What a creep, but he's lucky the cops didn't blow his head off."

"Maybe so, Ike, and I know you don't care much for policemen, but believe me it was a relief to see those blue lights last night."

"I suppose so."

"Anyway, my mom is trying to figure out how to protect the family. She thinks the guy needs some help with his drinking problem."

"I'd say," Ike said as he sipped more beer. According to a few things Theo had overheard, Ike had his own issues with drinking, and that was one reason his parents had little to do with him. That and the blowup of the law firm many years ago. The adults never talked about what happened, but Theo was determined to find out one day.

They talked some more. Theo said he had to go, since it was Tuesday and his family spent the evening at the homeless shelter.

6

By Thursday afternoon, the third day of testing, Theo's brain was fried, and he didn't care what happened with his scores. He left the school and rode his bike around town, trying to clear his head. At four, he met April at Guff's Yogurt Shop for his usual double serving of chocolate covered with crushed Oreos. April, a person who tried to avoid doing anything the same way twice and was always exploring, ordered a single of mixed boysenberry and mango. She ate less than half of it and offered the rest to Theo, who took one bite and slid it back across the table. They talked about how awful the testing was going and how they couldn't wait until Friday afternoon. They talked about the ninth grade. Theo was not looking forward to it at all. April was eager to move on and get out of middle school. She wanted the next few years to speed along so she could leave home. Theo thought that was so sad.

He eventually arrived at Boone & Boone, but with no homework to do he played video games in his office and got bored. Around five, his mother tapped on his door and asked him to step into the conference room. He said, "Sure, Mom, what's up?"

"You'll see," she said. "Follow me."

When he walked into the room he was startled to see Pete sitting at one end of the long table with his parents. Mr. Boone and Elsa were also seated. When Mrs. Boone and Theo sat down, she said, "Mr. Holland has something to say."

He slowly stood up, though standing was not necessary. He was obviously troubled and nervous. He cleared his throat, looked at each of them, and began, "Look, I'm just gonna come right out and say this. I have a drinking problem, and tomorrow I'm going to an alcohol treatment place for thirty days. Mrs. Boone here has worked out a deal with the police, and if I stop drinking and stay sober, all the charges will be dismissed. I promise I'm going to do that." His voice cracked, and he looked at Mrs. Holland, who was wiping tears from her cheeks. "I love my family and I'm not going to lose them. I promise." His voice cracked again. The guy was really struggling, and Theo felt sorry for him. However, he couldn't help but flash back to Monday night, or early Tuesday morning, the last time he had seen Mr. Holland, drunk and staggering around the front yard. What a change!

Theo glanced at Pete, who was also wiping his eyes.

Mr. Holland continued: "I want to apologize to all of you for what happened. I'm really embarrassed by it but just happy no one got hurt. I ask for your forgiveness." Each of the three Boones nodded their forgiveness. "And I want to thank Mrs. Boone for taking control and helping us out of this mess. I promise nothing like this will happen again, and I promise to get help and protect my family."

His hands were shaking and his eyes were moist. "Thank you," he said, and sat down.

Mrs. Boone said, "Your apology is accepted, and I'm just happy to do my job."

"Thank you," he said. The three Hollands were now holding hands.

"We will help any way we can," Mr. Boone said. The Hollands nodded awkwardly. The whole scene was awkward, and Theo had had enough. On the one hand, he felt sorry for Pete for having to suffer through his father's craziness, but on the other hand he was relieved that there might just be a happy ending.

They eventually stood and said thanks again, then good-bye. On the front porch, Theo shook hands with Pete and wished him luck. The Hollands walked down the front sidewalk together and disappeared down the street.

Since Mrs. Boone was a busy lawyer, and since cooking was not one of her favorite activities, the Boones dined out most nights. Monday was always Italian food at Robilio's. Tuesday they ate while volunteering at the homeless shelter. Wednesday was Chinese carryout, which was perhaps Theo's favorite because they ate on trays in the den and watched television. It was Judge's favorite too because he loved sweet-and-sour pork.

And Thursday meant roasted chicken at a small Turkish café. This Thursday, though, Theo really wasn't in the mood for it. He had a busy night ahead of him as he needed to carefully arrange his hiking and camping supplies. Mrs. Boone had a six o'clock appointment and would be working late, so Theo convinced his dad to go see the Dragon Lady again and pick up some carry-out.

After dinner, Theo hurried upstairs to his bedroom and began laying out his equipment and supplies. For Christmas and birthdays he always asked for scouting and camping gear. As an only child, he realized he was lucky to have more stuff than most kids, though he was careful to never show it. He found his "Ultralight Backpacking Checklist" and started an inventory. The Major was a fanatic about lightweight and efficient packing and believed that no backpack should weigh over thirty pounds. He would weigh each one at the VFW tomorrow before they boarded the bus.

Theo's backpack was a superlight, nylon contoured pack with padded straps, a hip belt, and eleven external pockets. It weighed three-and-a-half pounds. His tent was a quarter-dome one-person tent, also made of nylon and ultralight. It weighed three pounds and when erected would provide twenty square feet of floor area, more than enough room. His sleeping bag was an insulated, three-season bag that weighed two-and-a-half pounds and was fine for weather above thirty degrees. The weekend forecast was mild. The sleeping pad was a roll of foam that weighed ten ounces. The rain fly was nothing more than a sheet of plastic that weighed one pound, including hubbed poles.

The Major frowned on meals that had to be cooked because too many supplies were needed, so there was too much to carry. Instead, he favored ready-to-eat foods and energy bars. Theo had planned six meals: one for Friday dinner, three on Saturday, and breakfast and lunch on Sunday. With his allowance, he had purchased three packs of freeze-dried chicken and noodles, two packs of chili mac and cheese, two packs of breakfast waffles, and two packs of beef stroganoff with noodles. Just add hot water and the meals were ready to eat. He also had a dozen energy bars. It was probably a little too much, but it was also wise to have extra food. Out of the fifteen Scouts headed for the weekend, Theo knew that at least two would run out of food. His groceries weighed two-and-a-half pounds. His plastic cookset included a two-liter pot, two bowls, two mugs, a knife, fork, and spoon, all together weighing only one-and-a-half pounds.

Since they would be hiking a fixed trail, the Major said they would not have to worry about navigation. Theo looked at his checklist and crossed off the map, compass, and GPS. He also knew that the Major would carry a small GPS and a cell phone.

Back to the checklist: flashlight, batteries, lip balm, sunscreen, extra asthma inhaler, knife, first aid kit, water bottle, matches, fire starter, and toilet paper in a small waterproof container. His clothing consisted of what he would wear into the woods Friday afternoon, plus two shirts and one pair of pants, socks, underwear, a poncho for rain, a vest, and gloves. He had no plans to pack a toothbrush and toothpaste—what a waste of space! His hiking boots were waterproof, and since he was wearing them their weight didn't count. Only the gear that went into his backpack was included in the Major's thirty-pound limit.

With great care, Theo placed the gear and supplies into the backpack. As always, there wasn't a square inch to spare, but it zipped up without too much trouble. He hauled it downstairs, showed it proudly to his parents, who were reading in the library, then asked them if he could use their bathroom scale. The backpack weighed thirty-two pounds, and Theo hauled it back upstairs, unpacked it, laid everything out on his bed, read the checklist again, and argued with himself about what to delete. He was deep in thought and mumbling a lot, and Judge looked at him curiously. He removed a shirt, a pair of socks, and two packs of food. He removed the rain fly because the forecast was for clear skies, plus he figured he could just stay in his tent in the event of a shower.

Back downstairs, he was headed for the scale again when his mother said, as only a mother can, "Teddy, dear, do you really think you're going to be safe out there?"

His father said, "Come on, Marcella, we've already had this conversation."

Theo knew his mother was not about to veto his weekend, that she was just going through the motions of being a concerned mother, but he politely said, "Sure, Mom. This is no big deal. We're all experienced Scouts and you trust the Major, don't you?"

"I suppose," she said.

"He'll be fine," his father said. Theo suspected they were secretly planning a quiet weekend without him. He wouldn't be missed.

The second weigh-in was at thirty-and-a-half pounds. Theo decided to leave things alone. Surely the Major would bend on half a pound.

7

Friday morning, the last day of the dreadful tests. The ordeal was almost over, and Theo was so excited about the weekend he demolished his Cheerios and left home ten minutes early.

The mood was considerably lighter as the eighth graders gathered in the auditorium. Pete had a smile on his face, the first of the week. April smiled and nodded at Theo from across the room. The teachers passed out the exams, and at precisely nine o'clock they began. Theo attacked the test as never before, as if the clock would move faster if he kicked into high gear. It did not, but for the first time all week he felt comfortable with the material. The morning session was all about history, an easy subject for Theo. He nailed one question after another.

At 12:30, it was over. The proctor called "Time," thanked the students for their hard work and diligent efforts and on and on, and told them to go have lunch. At 1:30, they were dismissed early, and fifteen minutes later, Theo was at the VFW with the other Scouts, all chatty and excited and ready to go. His father had delivered his backpack and a change of clothes. The Major was barking orders here and there, going through his usual drill sergeant routine, but he, too, was eager to hit the road. He weighed each backpack—Theo's came in at thirty pounds, two ounces— and growled at Woody and Hardie who were two pounds over. They quickly unpacked, discarded a few items, and made the limit. All in all, the Major was pleased that his boys had packed so carefully. He went through a checklist to make sure each had included the essentials—primarily food and toilet paper—and told them to load up. They piled everything into the Troop 1440 bus, one bought from the school district and painted Army green, and by 2:30 they were leaving Strattenburg with the Major at the wheel and the fifteen Scouts whooping and hollering. They settled down once the town was behind them and most fell asleep.

Two hours later they rolled into the Sassaqua National Park. A ranger directed the Major to a spot to leave the bus, checked the boys into the register, showed them where the new trail began, and suggested a camping spot five miles in. The first stretch was easy and he was certain they could make it before dark. "Good luck," he said as they slung their backpacks onto their shoulders. As they hurried away, he said, "Watch out for the bears. They're everywhere."

The Major took the lead and set a furious pace. He was sixty years old, exercised every day, and could do more push-ups and sit-ups nonstop than any of his Scouts. Within twenty minutes, they were sweating and breathing heavy. But they pressed on as the shadows grew longer. Things were darker in the dense woods. The trail was narrow, in many places less than two feet wide, with gullies and ravines on both sides. They began a gradual incline that seemed to go on for miles, and when they reached the top the Sassaqua River could be seen in the distance. "We need to hurry," the Major said after a quick rest. The trail curled through the woods and went downhill. A few rays of fading sunlight lit the campsite as they arrived, and they hurriedly unpacked and got organized. The Major laid out a tight circle around a fire pit, built a fire, and began boiling water, barking orders nonstop. The boys quickly assembled their small tents.

Theo selected freeze-dried beef stroganoff for his evening dinner, and when mixed with hot water it was delicious.

Dessert was an energy bar, which tasted like rubber, but who really cared? He was deep in the woods, far from home, far away from school, and at that moment had nothing to worry about. The Major, whose backpack was slightly larger than the others and had not gone through the trial of being weighed, produced a bag of marshmallows. They roasted them on sticks and wiped out the entire bag as the Major told horror stories of campers being eaten by huge bears and vicious cougars and wild boar hogs.

He had a lot of stories, the best of which he seemed to save for those moments when he was deep in the woods with a bunch of city boys. Every story ended badly, at least for the campers, but the Scouts had learned over the years that they were all tall tales.

Nevertheless, given where they were, the stories set the tone for the evening. There were jokes, other tales from the Scouts, a few true stories about other camping misadventures, but as the night wore on and grew darker, every sound became ominous. The Scouts began to believe that they were being watched by all manner of hungry beasts, or even runaway criminals. Around nine o'clock, the Major called for lights-out, and they retreated to their tents, zipping the flies tightly.

Theo tucked himself into his sleeping bag, which was

warm and comfortable. He wasn't afraid. He'd camped enough with the Major to know that he would protect them. Instead, he savored the moment, listening to the sounds of the thick woods as his imagination went into overdrive. A bad week was ending in a wonderful way. Tomorrow would be a grand adventure.

He was thirteen and unwilling to grow older. The entire week had been about the future, about testing for placement in high school and the mysteries of the ninth grade. Theo liked where he was in life. He loved scouting and camping. He liked his school and his friends and teachers. He liked being a boy on a bike zipping around the town. If he got into trouble his excuse was always, "Hey, I'm just a kid." That worked most of the time.

Why couldn't a kid stay thirteen forever?

The forest grew still as the animals and beasts fell asleep. Theo, too, finally drifted away.

For the next two weeks, school life was normal as the eighth graders recovered from the ordeal of being tested. In fact, the tests were so unpleasant they were never discussed. But they were not forgotten. The scores would be ready "in about two weeks," according to Mr. Mount and the other teachers. As the days passed, a soft drumbeat began as the countdown gained momentum. Every student was convinced he or she had bombed the tests and would be sent straight to the "slow track," a fate that meant utter failure and embarrassment. A few, namely Woody, boasted of deliberately blowing the tests so they could be deemed dummies and practically ignored in high school. Mr. Mount said things didn't work that way. Those on the Remedial track received a lot of attention, as did those in Honors.

One morning in homeroom, Mr. Mount finally delivered the solemn news. "Hey, everybody, I have the test results." He was holding a thick file. Everyone stared at it and took a deep breath. He continued, "As I have explained, your scores are lumped into a pool with the eighth-grade scores from Central and East middle schools. Students who score in the top ten percent from the pool qualify for the Honors track next year at Stattenburg High. This year the magic number is ninety-one. If your overall score is ninety-one or better, then congratulations. If your score is sixty-three or below, then you qualify for some more interesting classes. If you're between sixty-three and ninety-one, you will be on what's called the Intermediate track. Any questions?"

No one said a word.

As he began passing out envelopes, he said, "I'm going to hand each of you your score in an envelope. This is a private matter, something to discuss with your parents and not to talk about during school. Understand?"

Right, Theo thought. Everyone will know everyone's score by lunch.

He opened the official-looking envelope with his full name printed on the front. There were a lot of numbers, but the most important one was at the bottom: Overall Score: ninety. He had failed to make Honors by one point.

Ike had told him that in life there's always someone

smarter, faster, stronger, and so on, so don't expect to be number one in everything. Just try your best and deal with the rest. Theo was not the smartest kid in his class. Chase was a genius, a mad scientist who aced every test with little effort. Joey studied hard and made perfect grades. Aaron was extremely bright and very lazy, but always did well on standardized tests. Theo figured he would land around number four or five if the class was ranked, which it was not. Still, though, it was a disappointment not to make Honors.

The room was silent until Woody said, "Hot dog! Stuck in the middle where I'll get lost in the crowd."

"That's enough, Woody," Mr. Mount said. "Please do not discuss your scores until you've talked to your parents." The bell rang, the boys hustled out of the room, and by the time they arrived at Spanish they knew that Chase, Joey, and Aaron had made Honors, and Theo had not. Darren would begin high school on the "slow track," which was no surprise to anyone but perhaps Darren himself. He looked devastated and near tears.

Madame Monique taught Spanish and was Theo's second-favorite teacher. After fifteen minutes, she realized the boys were not paying attention, that their minds were occupied with other matters, so she closed the textbook and gave them an easy written assignment to do in class.

Theo's father would be disappointed. His mother probably would not. She despised the tests to begin with. Ike would be nonchalant and tell him to study harder, to show the people who ran the schools that he could outwork everybody else. Why was Theo sitting in Spanish and worrying about what the adults would say? This irritated him. So much of his life was geared to pleasing his parents, his teachers, even Ike. Why couldn't he just do his homework, do his best on all his tests, and let his life run its course without worrying about the adults?

Second-period geometry wasn't much better. By then the students were openly talking about their scores and who made "it" and who didn't. Most seemed surprised that Theo had not done better.

At lunch he went to find April, but she was not in the cafeteria. He bumped into Pete, who looked as sad as Darren. He whispered to Theo that he had blown the tests and was headed for a rough start in the ninth grade. He said he might drop out, just like his father had quit in the tenth grade. Theo tried to offer encouragement, but it didn't work. Pete thanked him, said his dad was doing okay in rehab, and that things had settled down around the house.

As Theo walked across the playground, alone, he wondered how a kid like Pete was supposed to do well on the tests when his home life was in such turmoil. How can a student focus when his father is in and out of jail?

He found April in Ms. Bondurant's art room, and one look said it all. She was by herself, eating an apple, and when she saw Theo she began crying. He sat beside her and said, "Come on, April, it's not the end of the world. I didn't make it either, but we'll do fine anyway."

She bit her lip, wiped her cheeks, and said, "You didn't make it, Theo?"

"No. Almost. Missed it by a point."

"Me too." She clenched her jaws in an effort to stop crying. "It's just that the best art classes are for the Honors kids. That's all I want, Theo, to study art and to make art."

"And you will, April. Nothing can stop you from becoming a great artist. There'll be plenty of courses for you, and for me, and for everyone else. Strattenburg High School is one of the best in the state, for everybody. Let's get over this."

"What will your parents say?"

"I don't care. I swear I don't. It's not like they're sending us off to a reform school. We're going to do fine in high school."

"My mom won't care either. And, of course, my dad is rarely at home. At least your parents care what happens to you."

"Come on, April. We're going to be okay."

"I can't believe Hallie Kershaw made it. She's such a brat, and she's already bragging about it."

Hallie was the cutest and most popular girl in the eighth grade, and Theo, like most boys, had a secret crush on her. "Is that all you're eating for lunch?" he asked, nodding at the apple.

"Yes, you want some?"

"No thanks. I really want a taco. That's what they're serving today, so let's go eat a taco, okay?"

"Thanks, but I'll stay here. I just want to hide."

"Well, you can't hide, April. Life goes on."

They sat in silence for a moment or so. She said, "You know, Theo, I don't mean this in a bad way, but I feel better knowing that you didn't make it either. I mean, I wanted you to do well and all, so don't get me wrong. It's just that you're about the only close friend I have around here. I guess this means we'll have some of the same classes next year."

"I know, I know. My dad always says, 'Misery loves company.' So I understand. Right now we have a lot of company. Let's go get a taco."

"I'm not hungry."

"You're never hungry, but you have to eat."

"I don't want to see anyone. It's easier just to sit here and be miserable."

"Okay, be miserable then. How about we meet at Guff's for a frozen yogurt?"

"I don't have any money, Theo."

"Okay, then we'll call it a date and I'll treat. Four o'clock?"

"I guess."

"See you then."

Mrs. Boone looked at Theo's test summary and said nothing for a few minutes. Theo watched her face as he sat as low as possible in one of the two large leather chairs facing her desk. He tried to look pitiful, though he doubted she would be upset with him. Finally, she said, "One lousy point, and now they'll keep you away from the best classes in high school. I knew I hated these tests. Now I really understand why."

"Sorry, Mom," Theo said, though he really didn't feel that bad. "I'll make straight A's and show them."

"Attaboy. Now go tell your father."

Theo and Judge hustled up the stairs and found Mr. Boone at his desk. "Got some bad news, Dad," he said as he handed over his paperwork. Mr. Boone chewed the stem of his pipe as he frowned at the numbers. "What happened in science?" he asked.

"I don't know what happened, Dad. I did the best I could. Science has never been my favorite."

"Then you should work harder there. One lousy point. If you had worked harder, you would have made Honors."

"I really don't think it's the end of the world, Dad. Our high school has good teachers at every level."

"But, Theo, you should always strive for the best. This is disappointing."

"Sorry, Dad. I did the best I could. I've never done well on standardized tests, you know that."

"That's no excuse."

"Mom is not upset. Why should you be?"

"I'm not upset, just disappointed. And I'm not your mother. She thinks these tests are a waste of time. I happen to think they're very important. They measure how well the students are doing, and they keep the pressure on the teachers."

"I can still graduate from high school with high honors, and that's what I'll do. I'll show them."

"Did Chase make it?"

Chase's parents were best friends of the Boones. Theo almost blurted, "Why do you care about Chase?"—but bit his tongue. He knew there was competition between the parents, though he didn't really understand it. He said, "Of course he made it."

"Well, good for him. We'll discuss this later. I'm very busy right now."

Theo and Judge went to his office. He locked the door, fell into his chair, and stared at the wall. He could not remember the last time his father had said he was disappointed with something he'd done. It was a lousy feeling, and the longer he brooded the worse he felt.

Since it was Friday, the Boone family routine called for dinner at Malouf's, an ancient Lebanese restaurant owned by an old couple who liked to yell at each other. The Boones always ate fish and the meal was usually pleasant. But things would be different tonight. Things would be tense because Mr. Boone would say something about Theo blowing the tests, and Mrs. Boone would rush to his defense. They rarely agreed on issues or events, but they kept their little feuds civilized. Theo decided, as he stared at the wall and rubbed his dog's head, that he would remain in a foul mood. He would try his best to ruin dinner, and that would inspire his mother to go after his father.

He liked his plan. He and his mother would gang up on his dad and make him feel rotten.

At four, Theo left to meet April at Guff's.

9

As always, Theo slept late on Saturday morning, and when he finally ventured downstairs his mother was at the kitchen table, still in her robe, reading the morning newspaper and waiting for him. "How about some scrambled eggs and bacon, Teddy?"

"Sure. Thanks. Where's Dad?"

"He's running errands, said he'd be back at nine to pick you up. He's excited about playing golf for the first time in a month. It's a gorgeous day, a little on the cool side, but he's ready to go."

Dinner at Malouf's had been the disaster Theo wanted. His father again expressed his disappointment at Theo's performance on the tests. His mother disagreed sharply, and though they did not argue in public, they were pretty frosty with each other. Theo just pouted. The entire evening was tense, and Theo couldn't wait to get home and run to his room.

"So Dad's okay this morning?" Theo asked. His mother was at the stove, cracking eggs.

"Oh, sure, Theo. We're lawyers, we disagree and argue, but no one carries a grudge. We've also been married for twenty-five years and know how to get along."

"I don't like it when Dad's disappointed with me."

"Theo, your father and I are very proud of you. You do your best in everything—scouting, debate, golf, schoolwork. He is not disappointed."

"Well, that's not what he said."

"He said what he said, but he didn't say it very well. I think he has some regrets, and he wants to play golf and talk about it."

"Then I'm not sure I want to play."

"Be a sport. How many eggs?"

"Two for me, two for the dog."

"You might want to look at the newspaper and check out the headlines this morning."

"What's happened?"

"It's all about the test scores. The city schools did very well."

"Great. Just what I need." Theo reluctantly picked up

the *Strattenburg Daily News.* The lead story was a glowing report on how well the city's third, fifth, and eighth graders had performed on the standardized tests. Congratulations all around. Of particular importance was the impressive rise in scores at East Middle School. East was traditionally the weakest of the three middle schools in town, all three of which fed into Strattenburg High. The eighth graders at Strattenburg Middle and Central had always scored higher, with East dragging behind. There had even been a story about the school facing probation if it did not improve. East was on the far edge of town, and Theo knew very few kids who went there.

In the center of the front page was a large photo of Dr. Carmen Stoop, the city's superintendent of education. She was quoted saying all sorts of great things about the testing and the performance of "our" students. Theo had never met her, but she was often in the newspaper. He got the impression she was an important person, though her job was often controversial. She seemed to enjoy the moment a bit too much, at least in his opinion.

Under her photo was a graph comparing the eighth-grade results. Strattenburg and Central dead-even with East only a fraction behind. Next to it was a similar graph from the year before, with East far behind. Dr. Stoop congratulated the hard work being done at East and said the improvement was "amazing."

The bacon was frying and the kitchen suddenly smelled delicious. Judge was now standing by Mrs. Boone at the stove, begging as always.

"Good news for East, I guess," Theo said.

"Oh, I suppose," she said, skeptical as always. "I guess it means the teachers there finally figured out how to prepare the students for the tests. I doubt if the kids are any smarter. They just know how to take the tests."

"Mom, I'm kind of tired of this conversation."

"So am I." The toast popped out of the toaster. She spread butter on both pieces and placed them on Theo's plate. She added peach jam, his favorite, poured him a glass of grapefruit juice, and served both him and Judge.

"Thanks, Mom."

"You are very welcome, Teddy. Now enjoy breakfast while I go take a long, hot bath."

She would stay in the tub for an hour, something Theo would never understand. He had hated baths since the day he was born. He didn't care much for showers either, but there were few other options. There was something—what was the word? Unclean?—about sitting in a tub of hot water that was okay when the bath began but got dirtier as the ordeal progressed. At least in the shower the dirty water was washed away.

But he kept these thoughts to himself. Bathing was another reason he loved the camping trips. He could go unwashed for days and no one cared.

He heard his father's SUV roll to a stop in the garage. Judge, on cue, offered a lame growl as if he was always on guard and might attack at any moment, then he quickly returned to his eggs and bacon.

Mr. Boone entered the kitchen with a big smile and a hearty, "Well, good morning, Theo."

"Morning, Dad."

"Are you ready for golf?"

Only if we don't discuss the tests. "Sure."

As he walked by, he tousled Theo's hair and said, "It's a beautiful day. Hurry up."

Theo smiled. His dad was fine. All was well.

10

Late Sunday afternoon, Theo was in his room staring at his homework, bored, and thinking of something else to do. His phone beeped with a text from April: *Theo, we need to talk. Now. Urgent. Meet me at Guff's.*

Such a message from her only meant trouble. Her home life was not stable, and strange things happened there. He texted: *Okay. What is it?*

I'll tell u when I see u. Now!

Theo hustled down the stairs and told his mother he was meeting April for a frozen yogurt. Predictably, she said, "Okay, but aren't you eating too much of that stuff?"

His father, who was reading the *Sunday News,* piped in with, "It's just yogurt. Isn't that healthy?"

"It's full of sugar, Woods, and I think Theo is eating too much of it."

"I'll just have one scoop, okay?" Theo said, though he'd never had just one scoop and wasn't about to cut back now.

"Be home in time for dinner," she said. Sunday dinner was Theo's least favorite meal of the week because his mother prepared it. She had little interest in cooking, and her lack of experience was obvious.

"Sure, Mom. Be back in an hour." As he left the house, he made a mental note that his mother had not specifically told him to have only one scoop. He had made the offer, though halfheartedly, and she had ignored it. Therefore, at least in his opinion, he was free to order as much as he wanted. A kid in Theo's shoes, with two parents as lawyers, had to stay on his toes.

April was waiting in a rear booth, far away from anyone else. She had not ordered and seemed nervous. "What are you having?" Theo asked.

"Nothing."

"Okay, if you're having nothing, then I'm having nothing. And if we have nothing they'll ask us to leave."

"Okay, one scoop of lemon coconut."

"That sounds awful."

"Please."

Theo ordered one scoop for her and his standard two scoops of chocolate covered with crushed Oreos. If only his mother could see him now. He paid for them and took them to the booth. April offered a polite, "Thanks."

"So what's up?" he asked.

She ignored her dish and said, "I don't know where to start, Theo." She paused and thought for a second. She was not the least bit sad or frightened, as Theo was expecting. Instead, she seemed excited. "So last night my parents decided to go out for a fancy dinner because it's their anniversary. They never go out together, and I was happy for them. Happy until they told me that Janelle would be coming over to sit with me. I'm thirteen years old and they abandon me all the time, so I couldn't understand why all of a sudden I needed a sitter. But I didn't want to ruin their big evening, and besides Janelle is sort of an old friend. She's eighteen years old and she babysat a few times when I was younger. She lives down the street and is pretty cool. So Janelle came over, and we ordered a pizza and watched some old movies. She's a real chatterbox, and, to be honest, it was a lot fun. Sort of like having a big sister. My big sister, March, left a long time ago, and I realized how much I miss her. Anyway, Janelle asked me about the testing at school, and I told her I didn't quite make Honors. She didn't either when she was in the eighth grade, and says it's no big deal. But here's the dirt, Theo, and you have to swear you won't tell anyone."

Theo had a mouth full and just nodded. When he swallowed he said, "I swear."

"I mean, Theo, this is a big deal, and things might get ugly."

"Okay."

"And it might affect you and me, too."

"Okay."

"I mean, I couldn't believe it when she told me."

"Are you going to take a bite?"

"Later. Anyway, you gotta promise—"

"I've already promised, now get on with it."

"Okay." She glanced around suspiciously. Guff's was empty but for the two of them. The soda jerk was playing a game on her phone. April leaned in closer and said, "Here's the story. Janelle has an older sister, they call her Binky, and she teaches eighth-grade math at East Middle School. She's been there a couple of years and says the school has a lot of problems. Well, Binky told Janelle that this year a group of teachers at the school actually got together and changed the scores after the tests were given. They met at the school on the Saturday after the tests, the same day you were off hiking with the Scouts, and they got in a room, locked the door, and spent several hours erasing wrong answers and putting in the right ones."

Theo was about to shovel in another load of frozen yogurt when his spoon froze halfway to his mouth. He placed it back in the dish and stared at her.

"This is what she told me," April said. "Binky stopped by the school that Saturday to get a pair of sunglasses from her room. She saw their cars in the parking lot so she knew they were there. Later, one of the teachers that she knows well confided in her and told her the truth. Binky was shocked. This teacher feels rotten about what they did and is afraid they're gonna get caught. They did it because the school is headed for probation, and the teachers could also get probation, or maybe worse. So they cheated, Theo. The teachers think they're helping the kids by saving the school and so on."

"Holy smoke," Theo managed to mumble.

"Can you believe it?"

"No, I can't. This is crazy."

Slowly, April took a bite, a small one. Theo was too stunned to eat. He said, "You know what this means, don't you?"

"I think so."

"Well, it could mean that you and I and possibly several others who came close to making Honors got a raw deal because these teachers decided to cheat."

"That's what I thought."

"Who else knows about this?"

"I have no idea, but it must be a pretty big secret."

"How many teachers are involved?"

"Five or six."

"That's crazy. You never commit a crime with that many people involved. Somebody's bound to talk."

"A crime? Is this against the law?"

Theo paused and took a bite. He thought about this for a few seconds and said, "Don't know. I'm sure it could get them fired, but not so sure it's actually breaking the law. I'll have to do some research when I get back to the office."

"You sound like a real lawyer."

"I meant to. That's how I impress girls."

"Okay, then, if you're so smart tell me what we're going to do about this."

"Who said we have to do anything? If we complain to someone, we look like sore losers. It seems to me that this is a perfect example of something a couple of nosy kids should stay away from."

"Nonsense, Theo. Look, I know you and I know deep down inside you wanted to make Honors, you just won't admit it. At least I'm honest. I wanted it badly, and I'm really frustrated that I was not in the top ten percent. Both of us missed it by one point. Now we find out that there's a real good chance that some of the kids who did make it got their scores improved by their teachers. We can't just sit by and do nothing."

"What do you have in mind?"

"That's where you come in, Mr. Lawyer. What if you told your parents?"

"Why don't you tell your parents?"

"Seriously, Theo? My parents are crazy, you know that. They don't care what kind of classes I take or what grades I make."

"Must be nice."

"Well, it's not, believe me. I think you should tell your parents."

"They'd tell me to butt out."

"No they wouldn't, Theo. Your parents are lawyers who understand right from wrong, and they get ticked off when the wrong person wins. Your mother, especially. She never backs down from a good fight."

"I don't know. I still think it would sound like we're just

a couple of sore losers. And we don't know for sure that this story is true."

"No, we don't. So explain to me why Binky would make up such a crazy story and tell her sister."

"I can't explain that."

"No, you can't, and that's because the story is true. Look at what we do know for a fact: that East Middle School had a dramatic rise in its scores for eighth graders. In fact, Janelle said that in all their years of testing no school has seen such a big jump. Sounds pretty suspicious, right?"

"Yes, it does, I admit."

"Thank you. So are you going to tell your mother?"

"Look, April, this is a lot to swallow all at once. Give me some time. Let's sleep on it and have a chat tomorrow, okay?"

"Okay."

Theo finished his yogurt. April didn't like hers, so he finished it too. He'd never heard of lemon coconut but it wasn't that bad. When both dishes were empty, they left Guff's on their bikes. As Theo pedaled home, he was still trying to convince himself Binky's story was true. Eighth-grade teachers changing test answers?

After dinner, and while he was once again doodling with his homework, he did an online search into standardized tests. It didn't take long to find the ugly truth. In the past ten years, in at least four school districts across the country, teachers had been caught doing the same things Binky had described to Janelle.

Unbelievable.

On Monday at school, Theo managed to avoid April. He did not want to discuss the cheating scandal, if there really was one, because he was not about to get involved. And what could he do anyway? He was just a student, a thirteen-year-old kid. It was a problem for the adults to worry about. If the teachers at East had done something wrong, they would eventually be caught and punished.

He wasn't sticking his nose into the middle of it.

April, though, had other plans. She caught him at lunch on Tuesday and insisted they meet again at Guff's. Theo didn't want to but couldn't say no. His jeans were fitting a bit tight, and he was almost certain it wasn't just because he was a growing boy, so he ordered only one scoop. They hid in the same booth. April went for the blackberry swirl.

After two bites, she looked around suspiciously and said, "I have something to show you."

"Okay."

"I couldn't sleep Sunday night, so I decided to do this." She reached into her backpack and removed a plain white unmarked envelope, letter-sized. "What is it?" Theo asked as he opened it.

"Just read it," she said, somewhat proudly.

Theo removed a letter, printed on a sheet of white copy paper. It read:

> To Dr. Carmen Stoop, Superintendent of
> Strattenburg City Schools
>
> Dear Dr. Stoop:
>
> I am a concerned citizen. The recent rise in
> test scores at East Middle School, especially
> at the eighth-grade level, is very impressive.
> You said so yourself in an interview. But
> you should know the real story. On the
> Saturday after the tests were finished, a
> group of East Middle School eighth-grade
> teachers gathered at the school, got the tests,
> met behind a locked door, and began erasing

*wrong answers and replacing them with the
correct ones. I don't know the names of all the
teachers—there were five or six—but one was
a Mr. London and one was a Ms. Kovak.*

*I'm sure that if you examined these tests,
you would find a large number of erasures,
more than the usual.*

*This should be investigated immediately. If
not, I plan to send a copy of this letter to the
Strattenburg Daily News.*

Sincerely,

Anonymous

Theo read it twice, calmly refolded it, and said, "Nice letter.
Now, what are you going to do with it?"

"It's done. I mailed it yesterday and sent a copy of it
to Mr. Robert McNile, the attorney for the school board.
Found him on the website."

"You're kidding, right?"

"I'm dead serious."

"What about fingerprints?"

"I used gloves. Saw it once on television."

"Did you lick the stamp?"

"No."

"Did you lick the envelope?"

"No. Thought of that, too."

"Where did you mail it?"

"The post office on Main Street."

"There are about a dozen surveillance cameras there."

"And they video a thousand people a day."

"They can trace ink back to your printer."

"Don't be so sure about that, but I'm not worried. Why would they ever suspect me? There are seventy-five thousand people in this city."

Theo took a deep breath and looked away. She was still smiling, as if to say, "Aren't I clever?"

He said, "April, you can't accuse people of doing bad things if there's no proof. This was not a good idea. I wish you had discussed it with me."

"I was going to but you avoided me yesterday."

"You could have waited until today."

"I didn't want to wait. Something needs to be done, and it was pretty clear to me that you didn't want to get involved. Right?"

"Right. I did not want to get involved, and you should have left it alone."

The smile vanished and was replaced by a frown. "Look, Theo, what if this letter makes them look into the matter? They start digging and they find something. They find the cheating."

"Then what? They throw out the tests, and we have to do it all over again?"

"I don't know. I can't answer that. I guess they'll figure it out when they get there."

Theo took a couple of bites and tried to organize his thoughts. He said, "No one else knows about this, right?"

"Only you. I wouldn't dare tell anyone. Why are you so worried, Theo? Dr. Stoop and the lawyer will probably just ignore it anyway, but what if they take it seriously? You have to agree that this needs to at least be investigated. And if they dig into it and find nothing that'll be the end. But if the cheating really happened, and they discover it, then the letter was a good idea. Right?"

"I guess. I just don't like the idea of accusing people without all the facts."

"You're such a lawyer, Theo."

"Okay, I'm the lawyer, and you're the client. My advice to you is to bury this and not tell a soul. Never. Got it?"

"Got it. Stop worrying."

Theo slid the letter across the table. She said, "No, that's your copy."

"I don't want it."

Two days later, Theo bounded down the stairs with Judge at his heels and found his mother in the kitchen. She was decked out in a lovely maroon dress with matching heels, and Theo knew immediately that she was headed to court. She saved her finest attire for court and often complained that the female lawyers were expected to look sharp there while the men often looked like slobs. Theo didn't see it that way. He spent a lot of time in court-rooms and was of the opinion that all lawyers dressed up a bit when they were appearing before judges and juries.

"I have to be in court at nine, Theo," she said. "All day, and I'll probably be late for dinner."

"Sure, Mom. What's up?"

"A divorce trial. You might want to take a look at the

morning paper." Theo was pouring Cheerios into two bowls, in equal amounts. Judge often examined his bowl before he attacked it, just to make sure he received the same amount as Theo.

She pecked him on the cheek and said, "I'm off. Do you have lunch money?"

"Yes, ma'am."

"And your homework is done."

"All done, Mom."

"Have a great day, Teddy, and remember to keep smiling."

"You got it."

"Don't forget to lock up."

"Sure, Mom."

After she closed the door, Theo sat down for breakfast. He slid the newspaper over and looked at the front page. The headline read: "Questions Arise Over Testing." He forgot about his cereal and began reading. Citing an anonymous source, the reporter wrote that city school officials were looking into rumors that some of the test scores from the East Middle School eighth grade may have been tampered with. The reporter repeated what was already known, that the eighth-grade students there had shown a remarkable improvement from the year before, so much so that some suspicions had been aroused. What was even more suspicious was the fact that the folks who ran the schools were not talking. There was another photo of Dr. Carmen Stoop, and the reporter wrote that his efforts to speak with the superintendent had been denied. The school board attorney, Mr. Robert McNile, did not return his phone calls. The reporter tried to talk to several people but no one was willing. His unnamed source was saying that Dr. Stoop and Mr. McNile had received an anonymous tip that came in the form of an unsigned letter, and that this letter was stirring up questions about the scores being "altered."

The story had an aggressive tone to it and left no doubt that the journalist was not going away.

"Wow," Theo mumbled to himself as his appetite vanished. He read the story again and managed to choke down a couple of bites, then he hurriedly rinsed both bowls, forgot to brush his teeth, and said good-bye to Judge. The dog was not happy because he was being left at home. Usually, he rode to the office with Mrs. Boone, but occasionally he was forced to spend the day alone. This upset him. Theo spoke to him and promised to pick him up after school.

After second period, Theo sneaked into the library, opened his laptop, and checked the local news. There was an update. At nine that morning, Dr. Stoop had issued a statement in which she said the school board had hired "independent investigators" to look into the "rumors" regarding cheating at East Middle School.

The investigation was moving faster than the news about it. Dr. Stoop and her staff had, in fact, been suspicious not long after they had first seen the test scores. The improvements at East were almost too good to be true. However, they had accepted the scores, even said nice things about them, and really hoped there was nothing sinister behind them. Perhaps the scores were accurate and life would peacefully go on.

But the anonymous letter had floored them. The fact that whoever wrote it had been bold enough to name names— Mr. London and Ms. Kovak—forced Dr. Stoop to start asking questions. The attorney, Mr. McNile, advised her to immediately hire investigators from outside the school system and get to the bottom of it. Then somebody—they would never know who—leaked the story to the newspaper reporter, and the scandal was in the process of blowing up.

The investigators spent hours reviewing the tests. Their conclusion was obvious and simple: Yes, there were far more erasures on the eighth-grade tests than would appear to be normal. For example, in a typical two-hour exam on history, with fifty questions, the average test-taker would make five changes. He or she would erase the bubble for either *A*, *B*, *C*, *D*, or *E*, and fill in another bubble for the second, and correct choice, with a standard lead pencil. But for some of the eighth-grade exams at East, there were up

to fifteen erasures. Late Thursday afternoon, the investigators met with Dr. Stoop and her staff and delivered the bad
news. She told them to press on with all due speed. The
reporter was calling and things could get out of control.

On Friday, as Theo was hiding in the library and scanning
the Internet for news, the principal at East asked Ms. Emily
Kovak to please step into his office. Waiting for her were
the two investigators. They were pleasant and courteous and
said they just had a few routine questions. She was immediately terrified.

The first investigator asked, "Did you return to the school
on the Saturday after the testing was finished?"

"Well, I'm not sure if I remember."

"It was only three weeks ago. Do you often come to the
school on Saturdays?"

"Occasionally." She shot a frightened look at the principal, who was glaring at her as if she'd been caught stealing
some kid's lunch money.

"Then try real hard to remember if you came here on
that Saturday."

"I seem to recall that I did. Yes, the day after the tests
were over."

"And what was the purpose of your return?"

"I needed to pick up some homework to grade."

"I see. But the students had no homework that week, right? There's no homework during the standardized tests, am I correct?"

He looked at the principal who said, "That's correct."

Ms. Novak's shoulders sagged a bit, and she looked confused. She said, "It was some old homework that I had forgotten to grade. Where is this going?"

"Were there other teachers here that Saturday?"

"I don't recall seeing anyone," she said nervously.

"Was Mr. London here?"

She looked away, trying to appear as if she couldn't remember.

"Did you meet Mr. London and some other teachers here that Saturday?"

She couldn't recall. As the interview went on, she was able to remember less and less. The investigator never mentioned the possibility of changing test scores; that would come later. After half an hour, the principal asked her to stay in the room with him for a few minutes. The two investigators left and walked into the office next door where Mr. London was waiting nervously. The same questions were asked, the same denials offered. He, too, had a bad memory. But he was also rattled and did a lot of stuttering.

It was obvious to the investigators that the teachers, if they had in fact worked together and changed test scores, had formed a tight circle, and no one was willing to talk. But a school is a school, and word spread rapidly. By lunchtime, there were little groups of teachers in every hallway, whispering fearfully as the rumors roared through East Middle School.

Meanwhile, during lunch Theo found April in the cafeteria and sat next to her. They couldn't talk because other kids were close by, so they went for a walk on the playground. She had checked online and knew of the investigation. "I guess you're getting what you wanted," Theo said.

"Looks like it."

"You seem worried."

"Did I do the right thing, Theo? Please tell me I did."

"I don't know. If the investigation reveals a cheating scandal and the bad guys get punished, then you can say you did the right thing. If there's no scandal, then nothing bad happens to anyone, and your letter was harmless."

"So what's bothering you?"

"I don't know. It's just that I'm uneasy about why you did it. In some way it seems selfish. You felt cheated because you didn't make Honors, so you kind of stirred things up almost in revenge."

"I'm not selfish, Theo. That hurts my feelings."

"I'm sorry, but you asked."

"And it wasn't revenge. That sounds strange coming from you, a person who claims to always believe in justice. Let's say those teachers did what they did, and they're wrong, and because of their wrongdoing some students—yes, me and you and others—are being treated unfairly. Don't you think they should be exposed and punished?"

"Yes. And I'm not saying you are wrong, April. I'm just not sure what I think right now."

"I need you to be my friend, Theo."

"I'm always your friend. And besides, no one will ever know what you did, right?"

"Right."

13

Much to April's delight, Janelle called Saturday morning and asked if she wanted to go to the movies. They could watch a matinee and have a pizza afterward. April's father, Tom Finnemore, happened to be at home, which was rare, and was also in a good mood, which was even rarer. He said okay and gave her the money. The girls walked a few blocks to the cinema, watched a romantic comedy with Amy Poehler, and afterward walked to Santo's, a popular place claiming to serve "World-Famous Sicilian Pizza" near Stratten College.

April felt like the luckiest person in town. She was hanging out with an eighteen-year-old high school senior, a hip cool girl who would soon be leaving home and going away to college.

Over pizza, Janelle talked about her sister Binky and the storm brewing at East Middle School. Binky was worried about her friend and colleague, a teacher named Geneva Hull, one of the five teachers who may have cheated. Geneva was supposedly full of regrets for taking part in the scam and was worried sick about getting caught. The school had been "crawling" with investigators and reporters, and everyone was nervous. Even Binky and the teachers who were not involved were anxious. If the scandal blew up, the entire school would get a huge black eye. East had enough problems to begin with. This would probably seriously damage it and might even lead to its closing.

April suddenly had a knot in her stomach. A huge one. How much of this turmoil could be blamed on her? She had no idea, but she felt guilty about something.

Janelle knew that April was close friends with Theo, and that Theo's mother was a respected lawyer. Binky was wondering if Mrs. Boone might agree to a meeting with Geneva Hull.

Things were now really getting weird, April thought to herself. She nibbled on a slice of pizza but had no appetite. It was all very confusing: Theo, an eighth grader himself, had missed making the Honors track by one point, just like April, and now his mother might become the lawyer for one of the teachers who cheated and thus could be responsible for Theo not making the cut. April explained that she had no idea if Mrs. Boone would have any interest in taking such a case. It would be up to Geneva Hull to call her and inquire.

At that point, April was involved more deeply than she wanted to be. She wished she'd never heard of Binky or Geneva Hull or Mr. London or Ms. Novak. Why should she, of all people, now know the names of three of the five teachers? She wished she'd never sent the unsigned letter. She should have listened to Theo.

The Sunday edition of the *Strattenburg News* was, as always, two inches thick, with at least half of the bulk taken up by classified ads. This really irritated Mr. Boone, and he grumbled about the waste of good paper every Sunday morning. Mrs. Boone didn't help matters by egging things on with her usual, "I can't believe all of these classified ads." She would wink at Theo as she said this, then they would listen to Mr. Boone start complaining. The games adults played.

Theo rarely read the morning paper, but these days he was captivated by the news. Sure enough, the front page headline read: "Investigation Continues into East Middle School Test Scores." The same journalist, a guy who was obviously on a mission, reported that the private investigators hired by the school board were working around the clock to finish their work. They had interviewed many of the eighth-grade teachers—there were twenty-two in all—and claimed to be making "significant progress." However, several of the teachers were refusing to cooperate. Dr. Stoop was saying all the right things about her office's desire to pursue a thorough examination and so on. If wrongdoing was discovered, she promised to deal with it quickly and openly. There would be no secrets.

The article ended with some troubling words. Mr. Jack Hogan, the district attorney and chief prosecutor in criminal matters, was quoted as saying his office "was not involved at this time but watching things closely."

Theo read this and asked his father, "Dad, could these teachers get into serious trouble?"

Neither of his parents did criminal work. Mr. Boone was a real estate and business lawyer and rarely went to court. Mrs. Boone was a family lawyer who handled a lot of divorces. Occasionally one of her cases dragged her into contact with the police, like the Holland mess and the charges against Pete's father, but for the most part she avoided criminal law.

But since both were lawyers, they never failed to comment on anything related to the law. Mrs. Boone jumped in with, "Of course not. This is a school matter, and the teachers will be disciplined by the school board."

And since they rarely agreed on anything related to the law, Mr. Boone said, "I'm not so sure. If it's true, and these teachers were acting together, I can see them being charged with conspiracy. I'm not saying that's the right thing to do, but prosecutors love a good conspiracy and they often overreact."

"That's ridiculous, Woods," Mrs. Boone said. "These people aren't criminals. Maybe what they did was wrong, but they didn't break any laws."

"I didn't say they were criminals, but this could be a gray area. A lot of folks get burned in the gray areas."

Mrs. Boone shook her head but said nothing. Mr. Boone was right.

Theo asked, "What, exactly, is a conspiracy?"

Mr. Boone thought for a second and said, "It's when two or more people work together to do something unlawful or illegal. Nowadays, it's used by prosecutors to cover all sorts of bad behavior. I have a friend who's a criminal lawyer, and he says that conspiracy is often used when there's no clear crime involved. Would you agree, Marcella?"

"Perhaps," she said.

Theo was thinking about April and her unsigned letter.

If it in some way led to teachers being arrested and charged with crimes, April would never forgive herself. He knew she was reading everything in the newspaper and online, and she was probably worried sick.

Theo said, "I'm not feeling too well. I think I have an upset stomach."

Mr. Boone said, "What a surprise. It's Sunday morning, time to get ready for church, and you don't feel well. This seems to happen a lot."

Mrs. Boone said, "You look fine to me."

"Are we really going to brunch at the Baileys'?"

His mother said, "Why yes, Theo, it's the second Sunday of the month, and we always have brunch with our friends after church."

"Your friends, not mine. I'll be the only kid there, and I'll be bored out of my mind. I hate these brunches. Boring. All that adult talk. All those geezers grinning at me and asking me about school and trying to be funny, like I'm some cute little puppy who needs to be entertained. It's just awful."

His parents looked at each other, looks that meant they had actually heard him. Such looks were rare when discussing Boone family traditions. Their little rituals were important to them, or at least to his parents, and they didn't like to upset the structure of their lives.

Mrs. Boone finally said, "So what would you do for lunch?"

Something, anything. "I'll just come home and eat a sandwich. Please, Mom, let me skip it."

Mr. Boone exaggerated when he said, "Well, the Baileys will be disappointed."

Who cares about the Baileys? Theo said, "Oh, they'll get over it. You guys will have a great time with the other adults, and no one will miss me. Please."

She asked, "Well, what do you think, Woods?"

"I'd like to skip it myself," he blurted and laughed, though Mrs. Boone did not see the humor. She looked at Theo and said, "Okay, just this once."

Theo couldn't believe his luck. "Thanks, Mom!"

"Now run upstairs and get ready for church."

14

Theo arrived at school a few minutes early on Monday morning. He was met at the bike rack by Pete Holland, who had a smile on his face. As Theo was chaining his bike, Pete said, "My dad came home yesterday, Theo, a week early, and he's in great shape. He looks good and healthy, and he promised us again that he has quit drinking. We had a great time. Last night he took us out for pizza and subs, something we've never done before. I've never seen my parents smile and laugh so much."

"That's great to hear, Pete." They were walking slowly into the school.

"Things are gonna be tough for a while because he lost his job, but he thinks he can find another one pretty soon. He left home early this morning to look for work. He stopped smoking, too, and he promised there would never be alcohol or tobacco in our house. It's really hard to believe, Theo."

"I'm really happy for you, Pete."

"I just want to say thanks. Thanks to you for being my friend, and especially thanks to your mother. She's awesome, Theo."

"Happy to help, Pete. And you're right. She is awesome."

"And your dad, too."

"I'm very lucky, Pete."

They shook hands and went to their homerooms.

The week began as usual at Strattenburg Middle School. However, four miles away at East, things were off to a rocky start. As first period was beginning, the principal appeared in Mr. London's classroom and asked him to follow him to the office. Three investigators were waiting, and none of them was smiling. On the small conference table there was a suspicious-looking black box, with gauges and wires and cords running everywhere. It looked dangerous. Mr. London sat down and stared at it.

The principal said, "We are asking you to take a polygraph exam."

Mr. London looked bewildered and asked, "A lie detector?"

"That's correct," said an investigator.

"What's this all about?"

"I think you know," the principal replied.

An investigator said, "We're going to ask you about your involvement with Geneva Hull, Emily Novak, Tom Willingham, and Penn Norman on the day after the standardized testing was completed."

Mr. London dropped his head. They knew. They had all five names. His job was finished. His career was over. He covered his eyes with his hands and tried to maintain his composure. After a long, painful silence, he asked, "And what if I refuse the polygraph?"

The principal said, rather harshly, "You'll be suspended and escorted out of the school immediately."

"And if I take the test and flunk it?"

"I'm afraid this is one test you can't change."

His eyes were moist, and he wiped them. With a quivering lip, he said, "I'm not going to talk."

The principal said, "Then you are suspended until further notice. I'll follow you to your room to gather your things, and then to the parking lot. I'm sorry, Paul."

"So am I."

They left together, and as they walked down the empty hall, Mr. London asked, "What will I tell my students?"

The principal replied, "For now, just tell them you're not feeling well."

"That would be the truth."

They entered Mr. London's classroom, where an aide was chatting with the students. Mr. London said nothing as he grabbed his jacket and backpack. He refused to look at his kids as he left. The principal walked with him out of the building without a word and watched him drive away. He then returned to the hall and went straight to the classroom of Emily Novak. He apologized for the interruption and asked her to come with him to the main office. When she walked into the conference room and saw the strange device on the table, she assumed her day was taking a bad turn. "What's that?" she asked.

An investigator, the same one she had met the week before, said, "We are asking you to take a polygraph exam."

"Regarding what?"

The principal replied, "The standardized tests. We asked Paul London to submit himself to the polygraph. He refused and has been suspended. He just left. You're next, then Geneva Hull, Tom Willingham, and Penn Norman."

"The whole gang, huh?" she said without emotion, as if something like this was expected.

"Yes, Emily, the whole gang. We know what happened."

"Well, if you know what happened, then you don't need me to tell you. I'm not taking a lie detector test. I don't trust those things."

"Then you're suspended immediately. I'll escort you back to your class to gather your things, then to the parking lot."

As Paul London drove away from the school, he thought about either calling or texting Geneva Hull, who was not at school that morning. She was conveniently taking a sick day, as if she knew something bad was going down. Then he realized that his phone records might one day be examined. He wasn't sure who might check them, but using the phone at that moment suddenly seemed like a bad idea. Instead, he drove to Ms. Hull's apartment and knocked on her door. She was young, only twenty-nine, single, and lived alone. She answered the door, invited him in, and made a pot of coffee. For an hour they rehashed their mistakes and tried to think of what to do next. Mr. London had been teaching for twenty years and was beloved by his students. Ms. Hull had been at East for five years and was still uncertain if teaching would be her career. At that awful moment, it looked unlikely.

Both were emotional and frightened. They were certain

they would be fired and bewildered about what to do next.

For what it was worth, Mr. London took responsibility for the cheating scandal. Three years earlier, he had begun, on his own and by himself, changing test scores. His reasons at that time made sense, at least to him. He hated the tests to begin with, and he did not want his students labeled as slow learners. There were many lower income kids at East, and they were as bright as the other eighth graders in town. They just didn't have the same support at home and the same opportunities. He changed some scores, then he recruited Emily Novak and Tom Willingham, who were his good friends. They later added Penn Norman and Geneva to their little gang.

It all seemed so stupid now. They were bound to get caught. They had become too aggressive with their cheating and had left too wide a trail.

"You think we need a lawyer?" Geneva asked.

"I don't know," Paul replied. "I really can't afford one."

Ms. Hull's phone began buzzing. It was the principal. "I think I'll ignore that," she said.

"You can run but you can't hide," Mr. London said.

"I know."

Meanwhile, back at East, Tom Willingham and Penn Norman also declined to take a polygraph exam. By lunch, rumors were flying through the school, and everyone knew about the suspensions. In a text to all teachers, the principal called a faculty meeting at the end of the day to discuss the situation.

15

Elsa's desk was just inside the front door at Boone & Boone, and it was more of a command center than a reception area. With four incoming lines, she handled the phones with ease. Every caller received the same professional greeting, though a lot of calls were unwanted. She could immediately tell if a caller was shopping around for free legal advice, or had a bogus claim, or needed a lawyer for some type of work the Boones stayed away from, or was just one of the many nut jobs clogging up the lines. After thirty years, she had developed a sixth sense about who really needed help and who to avoid. She also handled the traffic: the clients who arrived early or late for appointments; the unexpected walk-ins; the door-to-door solicitors;

the endless parade of salesmen peddling legal supplies and law books; and the lawyers who were there for various meetings. She also balanced the schedules of everyone in the firm, including Theo and his dental and medical appointments. She kept up with birthdays, anniversaries, deadlines, and docket calls, and she sent flowers on behalf of the firm for funerals and burials. She made the coffee and made sure there was always a fresh pot. She fed Judge, who was always prowling for food. She reminded Mr. Boone to take his pills. She fussed at him for smoking his pipe, though everyone knew that was a waste of time. She handled the mail, ran to the bank, sometimes ordered lunch, cranked out routine correspondence, and could type faster than any legal secretary in town. In short, Elsa ran the firm, and for a lady in her seventies she had incredible energy.

She was typing away Monday afternoon when a young lady walked in without an appointment. She said her name was Geneva Hull, and she desperately needed to talk to Mrs. Marcella Boone. Elsa knew immediately that she was in trouble and needed help. Politely, she said, "Well, Mrs. Boone is very busy at the moment."

"I know. I should have called."

"May I ask what this is about?" Elsa asked without seeming to pry, though prying was exactly what she was doing.

"I'd rather not say," Ms. Hull replied.

"I understand, but Mrs. Boone specializes in family law, and there are many cases she does not take."

Ms. Hull looked around as if she needed extreme privacy, then swallowed hard and said, "I'm a schoolteacher, and I think I'm about to get fired."

"I see. And where do you teach?"

"At East Middle School."

Elsa quickly connected the dots and said, "If you don't mind waiting a bit, I'll see if Mrs. Boone has some time."

"Thank you."

Elsa handed her a sheet of paper and said, "Just have a seat in the conference room and fill out this questionnaire. It's just basic information. Would you like some coffee?"

"No thanks."

Fifteen minutes later, Elsa escorted Geneva Hull into Mrs. Boone's sleek and stylish office. Introductions were made and Elsa excused herself. Geneva took a seat, and Mrs. Boone eased into her swivel chair behind her uncluttered glass and chrome desk. With a professional smile, she began, "How can I help you?"

"I've never hired a lawyer before."

"Well, welcome to America. Everybody needs a lawyer at some point."

"I, uh, I think I'm about to be fired from my job at East Middle School."

"On what grounds?"

"The school thinks I'm involved in a cheating scandal, one that involves the standardized tests for eighth graders."

Mrs. Boone scribbled some notes and thought about this. "Well, Geneva, I'm not sure I should take your case. You see, I have a son who's in the eighth grade at Strattenburg."

"I know," she interrupted. "I've heard of Theo. Through a friend of a friend."

"I guess a lot of people know Theo. Anyway, Theo is a very bright kid and a good student, and he missed the Honors track by one point. Personally, I don't like the tests and I don't approve of the tracking system in place at the high school, and I know that Theo will do well in any school, at any level. But it seems as though you and I may have a conflict because of Theo and the tests results."

"I've thought about that, and I think that when the truth comes out it won't make any difference. The tests results will probably be thrown out, and, frankly, I don't know what will happen after that. I'll be gone, and maybe Theo will get another chance. Or maybe the scores for all the kids will be adjusted. I just don't know."

"Are you here to tell me the truth?"

Geneva paused and looked away. "I have a question."

"Okay."

"If you're my lawyer, anything I tell you stays in this room, right?"

"Absolutely."

"You can't tell anyone?"

"Never. A lawyer must keep her clients' secrets in strict confidence. The only exception is when the lawyer believes the client may do harm to others, but that's never happened in my career."

"Well, then, are you my lawyer?"

"If we can agree to keep Theo out of it, yes, I'll represent you."

"I can do that, but can you? You're his mother."

"I'm also a professional, Geneva. I keep my family life at home. Theo is going to be fine regardless."

"Will he know that I'm your client?"

"Normally, Theo does not know who my clients are, but there's always the chance he'll find out. It shouldn't matter. Why don't you tell me your story, and then we'll decide whether we should go forward together? And again, anything you tell me will be kept in confidence."

"Okay." Geneva took a deep breath and began with the events of that morning: the investigators and their polygraph;

the immediate suspensions of her four colleagues; her likely suspension, too. The more she talked the more she wanted to talk. Mrs. Boone listened carefully as she took a few notes.

Geneva eventually worked her way back to the beginning. "I'm sure you know that East has many low income kids. It's in that part of town, plus the school board tends to assign most new students to East. So we have a lot of immigrant families, a lot of kids using English as a second language and trying hard to learn it. We, the teachers, think it's unfair to place so many of these kids at East, but we're not in charge of that. And we love our kids. They show up every day with big smiles and happy hearts, ready to learn. They may not always have lunch money or have had something for breakfast, so we take care of them. No one goes hungry. I think we have to work harder as educators, because we often stay late to tutor kids who are struggling with the language. And we're there at night to meet with the parents, many of whom work two and three jobs and can't stop by the school during the day. Our students have to translate, which is often difficult. I have two Vietnamese kids in my class and their parents speak almost no English, but they care deeply and they want their kids to succeed. I guess what I'm saying is that the rules are a little different at East. And it's so frustrating to watch our kids struggle with the standardized tests, and then score lower than the others, and then get labeled as slow learners or dumb kids. They're not dumb, and they don't deserve to get stuck in Remedial in high school. So that's how it all started, Mrs. Boone. We did it. We're guilty. We're about to get fired, and our careers as teachers will be over. But we did it to help our kids and to save our school."

She finally paused and wiped her cheeks.

Mrs. Boone asked, "When did you first start changing the test scores?"

"Last year was my first year, and we didn't change that many. The school was facing probation after last year's results, so this year we changed a lot more. It's really weird because I think we knew we would eventually get caught, but we just did it anyway. Sounds crazy, doesn't it?"

"No, it doesn't. It's important, at least for the next few days, to stay away from the other teachers. I'll contact the principal in a few moments and get the terms of your suspension."

"You sound like my lawyer."

"I am. We'll get through this."

"Thanks."

On Tuesday morning, Theo (and Judge) lay in bed listening to the rain. He didn't want to start the day. The rain didn't bother him; there were more important things on his mind, primarily April. She was freaking out over the cheating scandal and terrified she would somehow get caught and exposed and sent to jail, all because of her anonymous letter. They had talked for almost an hour on the phone late the night before, with Theo trying to assure her she was not in trouble, she would not be caught, and so on. As the scandal was unfolding, it seemed pretty clear that the test scores from East were already raising suspicions before the arrival of the mysterious letter. Theo repeatedly told April that an investigation was likely without her involvement. He wasn't sure he really believed this (and who really knew?), but he had to say something to calm her. She was talking about running away, catching the bus at the downtown station, and riding it all the way to San Francisco. Theo reminded her that she had disappeared before, and he and Ike were lucky to find her. Things are going to be fine, he kept telling her. Just let the authorities finish their investigation.

But April was upset and would not listen to reason, or at least to Theo's version of it. She blamed herself for getting the teachers in trouble. What if they got fired? Their careers and lives would be ruined. But, Theo reminded her again and again, they were involved in a conspiracy to change scores, and if they are proven guilty they deserve to be punished.

Back and forth it went until Theo was exhausted. He did not look forward to another day of holding her hand and consoling her at school. And so he listened to the rain and skipped his shower. If he wet his hair and brushed his teeth his mother would never suspect that he had not bothered to properly bathe. He did this occasionally, and no one other than Judge ever knew about it. He turned the shower on, let the water run for a few minutes, got dressed, and finally went downstairs. His mother was in her spot in the den, reading and sipping coffee. Theo made breakfast for Judge and himself. He noticed the morning newspaper lying on the kitchen table, a clear sign that there was something important one or both of his parents wanted him to read. He took a bite of Cheerios and slowly pulled the newspaper closer. The front page headline read: "Five East Middle Teachers Suspended."

Oh boy. He chewed slowly but didn't taste anything. There were five photos in a row just above the fold. He zeroed in on Geneva Hull, the one who worked with Binky, who was Janelle's sister. Last night April had said she wished she'd never met Janelle. The girl talked too much, and now April had done something stupid.

According to the reporter, the five were suspected of working together to change test scores at the school, and so on. There was really nothing new, nothing Theo and April did not already know.

Mrs. Boone walked into the kitchen and sat across from Theo. She had that look, that serious motherly gaze that immediately told Theo that something heavy was on the way. Quickly, he tried to remember if he'd done anything wrong in the past few hours. Sure, he had just faked a shower, but how could she tell? He took another bite as if all was well, and with a mouthful said, "Got a busy day, Mom?"

As a lawyer, she enjoyed talking about how busy her

life was, how tight her schedule was, how many clients she had to see, or how many hours she would spend in court. Instead, she smiled and said, "We need to discuss something, something very important that cannot be repeated outside this house. Okay?"

"Sure, Mom." Whatever it was, it was far more serious than a fake shower.

She explained that she was now the lawyer for Geneva Hull, one of the five teachers, and she wanted him to know this because Ms. Hull's problems might in some way impact Theo and whatever eventually happened with the tests. Theo listened thoughtfully, even took another bite, and quickly realized that he was off the hook. He wasn't in trouble after all. He really didn't care what his mother did as Ms. Hull's lawyer.

Finally, he said, "Is that all?"

"Well, yes, Theo, but I just wanted you to know."

"Okay, now I know. Doesn't bother me, but just make sure we don't have to take those tests again."

"I can't promise anything, Theo. I have no control over what the school board decides to do about the tests."

For a split second, Theo wanted to tell her about April and the letter. The situation was getting out of control and quickly becoming something that the adults should deal with, not the kids. He'd done nothing wrong, right? And he was almost certain that April had done nothing wrong either. Maybe his mother should know everything. She always knew what to do in difficult situations.

But he'd made a promise to April, so he said nothing.

April skipped school. Theo couldn't find her anywhere, and she wouldn't answer his text messages. Missing school was not that unusual for her, and he guessed that she was hiding. He was also afraid she had done something stupid like run away. He worried about her all day, and after the final bell he biked to her house, but no one answered the door. He was late for Boy Scouts and received a stern warning from the Major. Since it was Tuesday, the Boones made their weekly visit to the homeless shelter on Highland Street. As always, Theo helped serve dinner to the folks who stayed there, and he helped the younger kids with their homework. Still no word from April.

Late that night, she finally sent a text. She was at home, hiding in her room, afraid to come out. He called but she wouldn't answer.

"Just great," he mumbled and turned off his light. An hour later he was still awake, but Judge was unconcerned. From under the bed he was practically snoring.

Wednesday would be one of those days that, when it was finally over, Theo would look back and wish he could have stayed in his room with the door locked. Just like April. But that would never happen in the Boone household because if he wasn't downstairs by 7:45 his mother would be upstairs banging on his door and barking orders.

Anyway, the eventful day began promptly at six a.m. when his phone began buzzing. He assumed it was April and debated whether he should answer it. But when he grabbed it, the caller ID revealed someone else: Ike. Ike was not known as an early riser, and for him to be calling at such an hour meant nothing but trouble.

"What's up?" Theo asked.

"What are you doing?" Ike asked in a scratchy voice.

"Well, I was sleeping until my phone starting making noises."

"Sorry. Look, Theo, I'm in a bit of a jam and I need your help. Right now."

When Theo got in trouble he usually called Ike, so he didn't hesitate. "Sure, Ike, where are you?"

"I'm in jail."

"Jail? Why are you in jail?"

"We'll talk about it later, but right now the most important thing is for me to get out. That's where I need your help. I need some cash to post a bond so I can get out, and I don't have enough cash with me. I want you to come down here to the jail, get my keys, and go to my office where I keep some cash."

"Okay, sure, Ike, whatever."

"And don't tell your parents. I'm really sorry about this, Theo, but I have no other choice. You know my office, and I can tell you where I keep stuff hidden."

"Okay, but if I leave now my parents will know I'm up to something."

"How soon can you leave?"

"I always leave around eight."

"Can you think of an excuse to leave earlier?"

"I'll think of something."

"Well, hurry up. When you get here ask for Officer Stu Peckinpaw."

"I know him."

"Okay. Hurry."

Theo stayed in bed for a moment and tried to organize his thoughts. He couldn't stand the thought of Ike being in jail and wondered what crime he had committed. It probably wasn't too serious if he could post a bond in cash. Serious crimes required thousands of dollars to get out.

If Theo started moving around now, taking a shower and getting dressed, his parents might hear him and wonder what was going on. So he stalled. He went online to see if any horrible crimes had been committed during the night. Nothing. Whatever Ike did to get himself arrested had not made it to the local news.

As always, Mr. Boone left at precisely seven a.m. Theo faked another shower, brushed his teeth, got dressed, and hustled downstairs. His mother was in the kitchen in her bathrobe. "You're up early this morning," she said.

He'd practiced his fib. "I know," he said with great frustration. "Mr. Mount wants the Debate Team to practice before class. He's tied up this afternoon."

She poured some coffee and said, "That's unusual."

"It really stinks if you ask me. It's not like we don't get enough school."

"Smile, Theo. These are the best days of your life. You should enjoy every moment at school."

"That's what they say."

She took her coffee and the newspaper and went to the den. Theo fixed two bowls of Cheerios and poured himself a glass of orange juice. He ate quickly, almost as fast as Judge, and at 7:15 was ready to go. He stuck his head in the den and said, "I'm off, Mom."

"Do you have lunch money?"

"Yes, and my homework is perfect. I'll smile all day long and make the world a brighter place."

"Love you, Teddy."

"Love you, Mom."

He grabbed his backpack, sprinted from the house, and hopped on his bike. Ten minutes later he walked into the police station. The jail was in the rear. He spoke to a couple of policemen and saw Officer Peckinpaw pouring coffee from a machine. He walked over and said, "Good morning."

Peckinpaw smiled and said, "Well, hello, Theo."

Peckinpaw was a veteran who patrolled downtown on foot. He liked to bark and swagger but was really a nice guy.

"Follow me," he said, and they disappeared into a maze of hallways. Peckinpaw opened the door to a small room and said, "Take a seat." Theo did and the door was closed. Five minutes later, Ike was brought in wearing handcuffs.

"Your lawyer is here," Peckinpaw said, and laughed as he removed the handcuffs. He pulled some keys out of a pocket and gave them to Ike. "You got five minutes," he said, and left the room.

"I've known that guy for a long time," Ike said. He looked across the small table and down at his nephew. Theo looked up and into the red eyes of his uncle. Ike usually looked tired in the mornings, even after sleeping late, but now he looked even worse. He said, "Listen, Theo, I hate this. You're the one person I would never want to see me in a place like this. I'm really embarrassed and feel awful about calling you."

"It's okay, Ike. I call you when I'm in trouble, right?"

"I guess so." He paused and took a deep breath. "I played poker last night with some friends, had a few beers, too many I guess. As I was driving home I sort of eased through a stop sign, didn't come to a complete stop, you know, at least according to the policeman, and he pulled me over. I was charged with drunk driving. Spent the night here. I'm really embarrassed, Theo."

"Don't worry about it, Ike, okay? I'm always your buddy."

"Thanks." He picked up the keys and selected one. "This opens my office door. Behind my desk is a credenza with four drawers." He showed him another key, a blue one. "This opens the bottom drawer on the left side. In it you'll find a small metal safe." He selected another key. "This opens the safe. Inside you'll find a tray of gold coins and a stack of one-hundred-dollar bills. Get five of them. My bond is set at five hundred dollars. I can post it in cash and get out of here this morning. I'm sorry, Theo, but there's no one else I can trust."

"No big deal, Ike. I'm happy to do it." Theo was secretly thrilled to be involved, but he was also sad that Ike had no one else he could trust.

"What about school?" Ike asked.

"I'll be late but it's happened before. Nothing to worry about. Should I tell Mom and Dad?"

"Tell them later, not now. The arrest will be a public record so there's no sense trying to hide anything. I'll go to court in a couple of weeks and take my punishment. They'll stick me with a big fine and take away my driver's license for a few months. I deserve it, so no complaints here. Guess I'll get me a bike, huh?"

"Bikes work."

"Take off. When you get back, find Peckinpaw and give him the money. He'll take care of the paperwork."

"Sure, Ike. Anything else?"

"No, not now. And thanks, Theo. I owe you a big one."

"You don't owe me anything, Ike. Happy to help."

Theo grabbed the keys and hustled out of the station. Minutes later, he parked in front of Ike's building, one that he owned. He rented the first floor to an old Greek couple who ran a deli, but it was too early for them. No one saw him bound up the stairs and unlock the door. Ike had no secretary, and his office was always a mess. His desk was covered with files and papers, most of which gave the appearance of not having been touched in years. Books were stacked on the floor. The garbage can was overflowing. The room smelled of stale cigar smoke. Theo flipped on a light, found the credenza, fiddled with the keys and opened it. The safe opened easily. He carefully avoided the gold coins and was impressed by the stacks of hundred-dollar bills Ike had stashed away. He plucked five from the pile, folded them carefully, and stuffed them in a pocket. He locked the safe and the drawer, turned off the light, and eased out of the office. He locked the front door and hopped on his bike. He had seen no one and was sure no one had seen him.

It was almost 8:30 when he returned to the police station. Peckinpaw was nowhere to be seen. Theo waited and waited, and finally took a seat in a folding chair. He sent a text message to Mr. Mount explaining that he would be late for class. Instead of a response from his teacher, he got a text from April. She was skipping school, too, and said she needed to talk. She needed a friend. Great.

Peckinpaw finally showed up a few minutes before nine. Theo gave him the cash and the keys. The officer explained that it would take about an hour for Ike to get out, and, in his opinion, Theo should go straight to school. Theo preferred to wait for his uncle, but if a police officer told him to go to school, then he really had no choice. Strattenburg had two truancy officers who patrolled the streets looking for kids playing hooky. If you were caught your life got complicated.

As he was leaving the police station, his phone vibrated. It was April and she wanted to talk. They met half an hour later at Truman Park, near downtown, and sat on a bench that was hidden by some trees.

"Why are you skipping school?" she asked. Theo told her Ike's story and finished with, "At least I have a good reason. Why are you skipping school?"

"I'll probably go tomorrow," she said. "Right now I'm

just too worried and upset. I had no right to stick my nose into their business like that."

This was the same conversation they'd had a dozen times already, and Theo was tired of it. "Look, April, what's done is done, and I'm not so sure what you did was a bad thing. It looks like the teachers are guilty. They cheated and now they have to face their punishment."

"You keep saying that but it doesn't make me feel any better."

"I don't know what else to say, April."

They sat for a long time and said nothing. Theo really wanted to go to school, to check with Mr. Mount and see how much trouble he was in. He also wanted to run by Ike's office and make sure the old guy was okay. But at that moment April needed a friend, and Theo was the nearest one.

He received a text from Mr. Mount: *Theo, u okay?*

He replied: *Ok here. C U later.*

April asked, "Who was that?"

"Mr. Mount. He's looking for me. We really should go to school."

"I'm not going to school today," she said, and that was final.

They sat for another five minutes without talking. Finally, she said, "You know what I want to do?"

"Not really."

"I want to have a picnic. Let's run by Gibson's Grocery near the college, get a couple of their corn dogs, and bike over to that spot above the river. No one will see us there, and we can have a quiet lunch."

"I think we should go to school."

"No, and besides, we've already missed half a day. Who cares? So we get in trouble. They can't shoot us or anything bad like that."

"My parents will shoot me."

"No they won't. They'll get mad and slap you on the wrist, but you're tough. You've been in enough trouble before. Please, Theo. I need a friend today."

He couldn't say no. Plus, he loved the corn dogs from the grill at Gibson's.

That afternoon, after he finally shook loose from April, Theo walked into the offices of Boone & Boone and said hello to Elsa. She asked how was school. He replied, "The usual. Is Mom in?"

"She's in court and your father has a client in his office."

Theo's plan was to march into his mother's office and admit to playing hooky all day. If she was busy and couldn't see him, he would go upstairs and confess to his father. But since both were occupied, he went to his office with Judge and closed the door, somewhat relieved that his big moment would be delayed. Now, he planned to announce it over dinner that night. After ten minutes he was bored. He left through the rear door and biked over to Ike's office.

Ike was busy at his desk, barefoot, with Bob Dylan playing quietly on the stereo, and an open can of beer near his phone. It was as if nothing had happened. He smiled at his nephew and said, "Great to see you, Theo."

"How are you doing?" Theo asked as he fell into an old chair.

"I'm fine. I feel lousy for what happened and for getting you involved. Believe me, Theo, you're the last person I'd ever want to see me in jail."

"It's okay, Ike. I've worried about you all day."

"Don't worry about me, Theo. I've been in worse trouble."

"So I've heard."

"You know, Theo, I'm thinking about giving up alcohol. I think I'd feel better."

Theo nodded at the can of beer and asked, "When do you plan to start?"

"That's what I can't decide. Maybe tomorrow. Maybe next Monday. I might even go away to one of those fancy rehab places for thirty days and do a complete dry out. Get it all out of my system and learn some new habits. I'm really embarrassed right now."

Theo wasn't sure what to say about this. Ike was the last person to be embarrassed about anything. He saw himself as a rebel with little regard for rules and laws and those in authority.

Theo said, "I skipped school all day, and I need to tell my parents about it. They will want to know why."

"You can tell them. I'll call Woods tomorrow and explain everything."

Mr. Boone and Ike rarely talked, and this had always bothered Theo. The fact that Ike would call Theo's father and talk about this was perhaps a good thing.

"Why did you skip all day?" Ike asked.

"It's a long story."

"I'm not that busy."

So Theo told him about April, and her anonymous letter, and the suspensions of the five teachers at East. Ike could be trusted with any secret. He seemed to like the idea that April nailed the cheaters with an anonymous letter.

18

When Theo returned to the office, his mother was standing at Elsa's desk, talking to Mr. Boone and Elsa and Vince, her paralegal. It was obvious that something bad had happened. For a split second, Theo thought maybe the school had called and reported him.

But it was far worse. That afternoon, the police had arrested Geneva Hull and the other four teachers. They were being charged with conspiracy and fraud, and Mrs. Boone was furious.

"These people are not criminals," she said more than once. "What is Jack Hogan doing? You'd think he and the police have more important crimes to prosecute, bigger criminals to go after. This is ridiculous."

Jack Hogan was the chief prosecutor and a well-respected lawyer. Theo had watched him in many trials.

Mr. Boone said, "Well, the important thing right now is to get Geneva out of jail."

"I know that. The poor girl is probably terrified. Picked up by the cops, handcuffed, thrown into the backseat of a patrol car, hauled off to jail. And I'm sure the police notified the reporters just to add to the embarrassment. This is an outrage."

"Has a bond been set?" Mr. Boone asked carefully. His wife was really upset, and he wanted to be supportive. For once, Elsa had nothing to say. Theo tried to hide in a corner, though he wasn't about to miss the drama.

"I don't know," Mrs. Boone said. "I'm going down to the jail right now to find out. See if you can get Henry Gantry on the phone and call me."

"Can I go with you?" Theo asked. "Maybe I can help."

"I don't see any way you can help matters, Theo," his mother said.

"Probably not, but I'd hate to miss all the fun."

"This is not fun, Theo," she scolded. "This is an extremely important matter, and an outrage."

"I'll stay out of the way. I've already been there once today."

All four froze and looked at him. He said, "It's a long story, for later."

"I don't have time for a story," Mrs. Boone replied. She threw up her hands and walked to her office. Seconds later, she came out with her briefcase and stomped out the front door. Vince followed her. And Theo decided to follow, too. He wasn't sure how far he would get, but he was willing to try. What did he have to lose? Mrs. Boone got behind the wheel of her car and slammed the door. Vince hopped into the front passenger's seat. Theo crawled into the backseat and waited for his mother to order him out. She did not. She drove fast and recklessly to Main Street and parked illegally, as if she was just looking for a fight. Vince and Theo followed her into the police station, and she barked at the first officer she encountered.

"My name is Marcella Boone, attorney-at-law, and I represent Geneva Hull, who was arrested about an hour ago. I demand to see her immediately!"

Theo could not remember a time when he'd seen his mother this angry. Luckily, there were no reporters hanging around.

There were a few other cops milling about, and they disappeared into thin air. The first officer said, "Well, uh, sure, Mrs. Boone. I think you need to see the head jailer, just down the hall."

"What's his name?" she demanded. Mrs. Boone handled few criminal cases and as far as Theo knew had never been to the jail. At the moment, though, that didn't matter.

"Officer Brock."

As they headed toward the jail area, Officer Stu Peckinpaw came around a corner, saw Theo, smiled, and said, "Well, hello, Theo. You can't stay away from this place, can you?" Mrs. Boone and Vince stopped and stared.

"It's a long story," Theo said, then quickly had an idea. "Say, look, Officer, this is my mother, and we need some help." Introductions were quickly made, and the officer volunteered to help. He led them down the hall to the jailer's desk. As they walked, Mrs. Boone said, "What was that all about?"

Theo replied, "I'll tell you later. Another long story."

Officer Brock was very helpful and informed them that Geneva Hull and the other four teachers were being "processed," which meant they were being mug-shot, fingerprinted, and would soon be placed in cells. Each had a bond of ten thousand dollars.

"Ten thousand dollars!" Mrs. Boone practically yelled. "That's outrageous. These are schoolteachers, not criminals."

Officer Brock said, "Maybe so, ma'am, but they were arrested under a warrant, and that warrant says the bond is ten thousand dollars. I can't change that."

"Well I can," she said. She looked at Vince and said, "Get Judge Gantry on the phone." Vince grabbed his phone and made the call. Mrs. Boone demanded, "When can I see my client?"

"Uh, well, I'm not sure."

"I demand to see my client as soon as possible."

"Yes, ma'am. I'll do what I can."

Vince handed over his phone and said, "He's on the line."

She grabbed it and said, "Henry, this is Marcella. I'm sorry, Judge Gantry. They've arrested the five teachers and are holding them on ten-thousand-dollars bond each. That's an outrageous sum of money, and I want it reduced." She listened for a moment, then asked, "Are you in your office? Fine, I'll be there in ten minutes."

She gave the phone back to Vince and said to Officer Brock, "We'll be back." Vince and Theo followed her out of the building, onto the sidewalk, and down Main Street. She walked fast, her heels clicking away, and Theo had to practically jog to keep up. They entered the courthouse, took the elevator to the second floor, and sprinted to Judge Gantry's office. His secretary, Mrs. Hardy, was Theo's favorite in the entire courthouse, and she was waiting. She led them into his chambers and closed the door behind them. Everyone said hello, how you doing, and so on, and then Judge Gantry looked at Theo. "What are you doing here?"

"That's a good question," his mother said.

"I'm a paralegal today," Theo said with a smile.

Mrs. Boone wasted no time. "Judge, I represent one of the teachers. All five have been arrested and are currently at the jail posing for their mug shots and being fingerprinted like common criminals. This is an outrage, and I want them released immediately."

Theo watched the judge's face, and at that moment there was no doubt his mother would get exactly what she wanted. His parents and Henry Gantry had been friends for many years. She was angry, upset, and she was right.

Judge Gantry said, "This case has not been assigned to me, and I know very little about it, only what I've read in the newspaper."

Mrs. Boone said, "Well, it's some sort of crazy conspiracy charge that Jack Hogan has cooked up. The teachers have been suspended and will probably be fired. But they are not criminals."

Vince had picked up some paperwork at the jail. He flipped through it and said, "The bond was set by the city court judge, Your Honor, but the case will be assigned to your court. We can make an oral motion to reduce the bond."

"I know that," Judge Gantry said politely. Theo had never seen him ruffled or upset.

"Then I make an oral motion to reduce the bond for all five," Mrs. Boone said.

"What do you have in mind?"

"Why not a simple recognition bond?" Vince asked.

"Exactly," said Mrs. Boone. "These people pose no risk of running away. They'll show up in court when they're supposed to. I guarantee it. Just release them on their own recognizance. They don't have the money to go through a bail bondsman, and it's so unnecessary anyway. I want them out of jail right now, Henry. Is that clear?"

"Relax, Marcella."

"No, I will not relax until they are out of jail. And once they're out, I'll file a motion to dismiss these ridiculous charges. Just wait until I have a chat with Jack Hogan."

"I'd like to witness that conversation," Judge Gantry said with a smile.

"Please, Henry, you know I'm right," she said.

"Okay. So ordered. I'll call the jail."

"Thank you, Henry."

"And thank you, Marcella. Please say hello to Woods."

They marched out of his office, past Mrs. Hardy, down the hallway and the stairs, out of the building, and back to the police station. It took an hour to shuffle the paperwork, even with Mrs. Boone glaring at Officer Brock and snapping at anything he said. Finally, a door opened and Geneva Hull, Tom Willingham, Penn Norman, Paul London, and Emily Novak emerged, free to go. Geneva started crying when she saw Mrs. Boone, who huddled with them for a few minutes and told them what had happened. Theo and Vince drifted away.

It was dark when they left the police station. Theo's day had started there, just as it was ending there. As he got in the car and they drove away, he said, "That was pretty awesome, Mom. Thanks for letting me tag along."

"Don't mention it, but we do have a few things to talk about."

"Yes, we do."

Over Chinese carryout, his parents decided that he should arrive early in Mrs. Gladwell's office on Thursday morning and admit to skipping school. He would take his punishment without complaining. He didn't argue with this decision. The mood was somber, and Mrs. Boone barely touched her food. She was still upset and gunning for Jack Hogan. Mr. Boone thought it was admirable for Theo to help Ike but didn't like the fact that he had fibbed to his mother about leaving the house early for debate practice. Theo acknowledged he was wrong and apologized, but pushed back a bit by saying he had no choice. Normally, his mother would have had plenty to say about the fib, but she was preoccupied with more important matters.

Theo described the rest of the day as an exercise in baby-sitting. April was also skipping school and needed someone to lean on. Theo did not tell his parents why. He had made a promise to April. Both seemed suspicious about his story. He felt like he was dodging bullets, and his head was spinning in so many directions it began to ache. His primary concern was April. What would she do when she heard the news that the teachers had been arrested? Getting suspended was bad enough, now this. She would blame herself and threaten to do something crazy.

Later, in his room, he called and texted her, but she did not answer.

19

At eight Thursday morning, Theo walked into the school office and said hello to Miss Gloria, the school secretary. She missed nothing and quickly said, "I see you were absent yesterday. Everything okay?"

She was nosy and often pried into private matters. "All is well," Theo said, "but I need to see Mrs. Gladwell."

"About what?"

Maybe it's none of your business, Theo thought, but he managed to smile and be polite. "My parents," he said.

"Oh dear. I hope nothing is wrong."

"They're fine."

He took a seat in the reception area and tried to ignore her. The phone rang and she answered it. Mrs. Gladwell arrived, in her usual early morning frenzy, and said hello. "Gotta minute?" Theo asked.

"Sure, Theo. What's going on?"

They went into her office and closed the door. Theo took a seat and announced, "I skipped school yesterday, all day. I have no excuse."

"Yes, I saw your name on the absentee list. Mr. Mount said you sent a text but never showed up. That's not like you, Theo."

"I'm sorry."

"And you've told your parents?"

"Yes. Last night. They are not happy. I can't play golf for a month, and here I am in your office, waiting for my punishment."

"Very well. Let's do an extra hour of study hall after classes for the next five days. Fair enough?"

"Whatever you say," Theo said.

"Okay. Now scoot along. I have a busy morning."

Not bad, Theo thought, as he sprinted by Miss Gloria's desk and out the door.

During morning recess, he found April on the playground. He was relieved she was at school. Her punishment for skipping was nothing because her mother had sent a note saying she'd been ill. That wasn't fair, but he didn't have time to dwell on it. She informed him that she had written a letter to Dr. Carmen Stoop, the school superintendent, and in the letter she admitted being the anonymous informant. She admitted everything and apologized for getting involved.

"Don't send that letter," Theo said as firmly as possible.

"I'm going to. This is all my fault, and I feel terrible."

"Don't send that letter. It doesn't help anyone, especially you. It will just make your life more complicated, and it could also cause trouble for Janelle and her sister Binky."

"I'm sorry, Theo. I disagree."

"Look, April, the first letter was a mistake, right? You sent it without talking to me first. This other letter will just make things worse."

"I disagree."

"Come on, April, you always say you trust me when it comes to the law, right?"

"I suppose."

"What do you mean, 'You suppose'? Do you trust me or not?"

"Yes."

"Then don't send that letter until I read it, okay?"

"I'll think about it."

During third-period Government class, Mr. Mount began, as he often did, with a current topic by saying, "Let's talk about the arrests yesterday of the five teachers from East Middle School. Who thinks they should be prosecuted and put on trial?"

Theo wanted to crawl under his desk. No one in the room had a clue that he was so thoroughly involved in the mess. He vowed to keep his mouth shut.

Woody, he with the quick trigger, said, "Sure. They caught 'em cheating, and now they have to pay the price."

Justin disagreed. "What law did they break? If they did it, then they were wrong, no question about it. They should be fired, but they're not criminals."

Brandon asked, "Is cheating always against the law? I mean, if we cheat on a test, are we breaking the law? I don't think so."

Edward said, "My mom says they're going to throw out all the tests and make us do it again. Now, that's a crime. If that happens, then I think they should go to jail for a long time."

Darren said, "My dad says the whole idea of testing is bogus to begin with. Why allow some kids in high school to get smaller classes and better teachers? Why shouldn't we all be treated the same?"

Mr. Mount was smiling because he'd hit a hot button. He said, "Okay, good points, but let's stay away from the tests for a minute and talk about the arrests, prosecution, and possible jail time for teachers. It strikes me as a bad idea."

Brandon said, "Okay, do you think cheating is always a crime?"

"Of course not. It's always wrong and some forms of cheating are clearly against the law. For example, if you cheat on your income taxes, the IRS can charge you with a crime. If you cheat on an application for a home loan, you could probably be prosecuted. But cheating on a test in school is not a crime."

"Now you tell us," Woody said, and got a few laughs.

"Oh, it's wrong," Mr. Mount said. "You would be punished, maybe suspended or expelled."

Chase asked, "So, Mr. Mount, what do you think should happen to the teachers?"

"I'm a teacher, so I guess I'm sympathetic to them. But I want to know what you think."

Mr. Mount looked at Theo, who quickly looked away. He let it pass, said nothing, and tried to lie low. The debate raged for half an hour, and Theo managed to keep his mouth shut.

20

Theo was able to avoid controversy and conflict for the rest of the day, but as he was leaving school, after an extra hour in study hall, a seventh grader named Byron caught him at the bike rack. It was obvious Byron had been hanging around, waiting on Theo. He looked nervous and spoke rapidly.

"I need some help, Theo," he said.

Theo was in no mood to help and just wanted to go hide in his office. But the kid looked pitiful. "Sure, what's up?"

"Well, somebody told me you know all about Animal Court, and I'm in some pretty big trouble. Not really me, you know, but my family has a pet that's causing some problems."

"What kind of pet?"

"An otter."

"An otter?"

"Yep. We live on the edge of town in an area where there are a bunch of small farms close together. We have a couple of ponds and some streams, and for the past two years this otter has been hanging around them. Do you know anything about otters?"

"Not really," Theo replied with hesitation. He had a feeling that he was about to learn a lot about otters.

"Well, otters are very friendly little fellas, and this otter—we call him Otto—has sort of become a family pet. He hangs around the pond and sometimes he comes up to the house. We leave cat food out for him every night. Last year my dad even took him to the vet when he got sick. So, Otto is a little guy that we like a lot."

"Otto the otter?"

"Yep."

"And why is Otto in trouble?"

"Well, you see, there's this family across the road, the Murrays, and they're nice people and all, or they used to be nice anyway, but they're kinda ticked off at us right now because the Murrays are really into gardening and stuff like that. Their place looks a lot better than ours. Back behind their house they have this fancy little pond—they call it a water garden—where they keep these big fat goldfish called koi. Are you familiar with koi?"

"No."

"They're these big ornamental fish; I think they come from the carp family. They're beautiful, red and orange and white. We used to go over all the time, back when the families were speaking, and look at their koi. We'd feed them, too. Anyway, it looks like Otto has discovered their pond because a bunch of them were found dead, stripped down to the bones."

"Otto has been eating the koi?"

"I guess so. They started complaining about a month ago, really upset. Mr. Murray threatened to shoot Otto if he caught him in the backyard. He didn't catch him, but he kept finding dead koi that had been eaten. It's a real mess. Then last week Mr. Murray called the house, yelling and cussing, and said he had set up a motion-activated video camera with night-vision stuff, and he caught Otto eating his koi. He's got a video. Then he filed a complaint in Animal Court, and we're supposed to have a hearing this afternoon."

"This afternoon? It's almost five o'clock now."

"I know. We're not sure what to do. My dad doesn't want

to hire a lawyer, and I was thinking maybe you could help us."

Theo loved Animal Court and went there as often as possible, often pretending to be a lawyer. In Animal Court, lawyers were not required; the parties were allowed to represent themselves. Judge Yeck was a friend. Theo considered the situation and said, "Let's go."

Ten minutes later, Theo slid to a stop in front of the courthouse on Main Street. He ran to the basement and found a small empty room where lawyers sometimes met with their clients. He quickly pulled out his laptop and went to Google.

He had watched dozens of trials, and in doing so had learned the lesson that great lawyers leave nothing to chance. They succeed because they spend hours in preparation before they get inside the courtroom. He didn't have much time, but he had to prepare. He skimmed the Wikipedia pages for otters, then the ones for koi. After a few minutes he raced to the other end of the basement where Judge Yeck conducted Animal Court four afternoons each week. In the hallway, Byron was waiting with his father. Quick introductions were made. Mr. Kerr said, "We got the otter outside in my truck, if you'd like to see him."

"He's very cute and makes a good impression," Byron added.

"He's here?" Theo asked.

"Yep. Billy's got him in a cage."

Theo thought for a second and said, "Probably not. Let's not tell anyone that Otto has come to town."

"Whatever," Mr. Kerr said. "You're the lawyer, I guess."

They went inside, sat in folding chairs, and listened in amusement as two neighbors argued over a barking dog. Evidently, they had been there for some time because Judge Yeck looked extremely bored. He finally raised both hands and said, "This is the third time we've sat here and argued over this noisy dog. I prefer not to do so again. Mr. Dumas, you either put a muzzle on your dog, or keep him inside, or get rid of him altogether. I have no sympathy for a dog that barks all night and keeps the neighbors awake. Do you understand?"

"I can't keep him in, Judge, because he'll just bark all night in the house."

"Too bad. That's your problem, but it should not be your neighbors' problem. I want the dog shut up, or I'll have no choice but to put him down."

"Can you do that?" Mr. Dumas asked.

"I certainly can. I have the authority, vested in me by city ordinance, to order the extermination of any animal inside the city limits. I'll show you the law if you don't believe me."

Theo had read the ordinance and knew it well. He also knew that Judge Yeck had handed down the death sentence to only one animal, a rabid dog that had bitten two people. He liked to talk tough, like a lot of judges, but deep down inside he really loved animals.

Theo also suspected the judge would take a dim view of Otto's nighttime raids into the Murrays' water garden, but he knew Otto's life was probably safe, for now anyway.

When the barking case was over, four people left the room, none of them happy. Judge Yeck looked at the remaining spectators and said, "Well, hello, Theo. Nice to see you as always. Are you involved in this last case, the hungry otter?"

"Yes, sir. And hello to you, too."

"Okay. I'll ask Mr. Murray and Mr. Kerr to come forward." The two men walked a few steps and sat at the opposing tables. Mr. Murray pointed at Theo and looked at the judge. "Is he a lawyer?"

"Well, sort of," replied the judge.

"Well, I don't have a lawyer. Do I need one?"

"Not really. I can do a pretty good job of finding the truth, with or without lawyers."

"Doesn't seem fair," Mr. Murray mumbled.

"I'll keep it fair," Judge Yeck said rather sternly. "You

filed the complaint, Mr. Murray, so you'll go first. How many witnesses do you have?"

"Just me."

"Okay. Keep your seat and raise your right hand. Do you swear to tell the truth?"

"I do."

"Then tell us what happened."

Mr. Murray shifted his weight and cleared his throat. "Well, Judge, I got this real nice water garden out back, got it landscaped and all, with lily pads and such. I spend a lot of time in the yard. About three years ago I started buying koi. Are you familiar with koi?"

"Sort of."

"Fancy name for big fat goldfish. I think they originated in Japan a long time ago. There are a lot of varieties, lots of sizes and colors, and, well, they're just beautiful in the water garden. They live forever, that is unless some damned otter comes along and raids the pond."

"I don't allow foul language in my courtroom, Mr. Murray."

"Sorry. So I stocked the pond with a lot of koi. At one time I had close to a hundred. We love the fish. My grandkids love them. They're just beautiful, and very hearty. Doesn't matter how cold or hot it gets. They survive. I have enlarged some photographs if you'd like to see them."

"Sure."

Mr. Murray handed the judge three large photos of the koi in the water garden. He had a photo of his house and the Kerrs'. He was prepared, and Theo envied the time he had had to get ready for trial.

"Please continue," Judge Yeck said.

"Yes, sir. Well about a month ago I went to feed the koi—got to feed 'em twice a day—and I was horrified to see some of them had been eaten. Something had attacked them in the water garden, dragged 'em out, and devoured them. Nothing but a few heads and a bunch of bones were left. I counted four of my koi dead. You wanna see?"

"Sure."

Another large photo revealed the carnage. Judge Yeck studied it, then handed it to Theo, who gave it back to Mr. Murray.

"Please continue."

"I didn't know what to do. The next night I sat on the back porch till midnight, just waiting and watching. I figured whatever varmint did it had such a good time that he was bound to come back. Then I fell asleep. Sure enough, next morning I ran out there and there were three more dead koi. Slaughtered. I looked for teeth marks and footprints but couldn't see anything. So I called John from across the road—"

"That's Mr. Kerr?"

"Yes, sir, and I asked him if he had noticed any dead fish around his ponds. Got two ponds over there, and he said no. So I asked him about his otter. You see, Judge, they've been keeping this otter around their house for a couple of years now. He's like a real pet. They even got a name for him. Kids play with him and all. He comes and goes as he pleases, and I suspected he might be involved with my koi. I've never seen him in my backyard, but otters usually move around at night. Two days later, I found two more dead koi. I called John Kerr again, and he got pretty irritated. Like I was accusing him of something. I guess I was, come to think of it. He said he didn't know what the otter was doing at night, wasn't his job to stay up and watch the little varmint. So a week or two went by with no more attacks. I was hoping it was over, but no. One day I found some more dead koi. Then some more. So last week I bought a video camera, one with night vision and activated by motion, and, sure enough, it caught their otter sneaking over and slithering into my water garden. Got the video right here."

"Let's roll the tape," Judge Yeck said.

Mr. Murray opened a laptop and placed it on the judge's desk. Theo and Mr. Kerr got up and walked closer. The images were remarkably clear. An otter, presumably Otto, came into view, seemed to stop and look around, then eased into the pond and went underwater. Seconds later he emerged with a fat koi in his mouth. He climbed out of the water garden and began chomping on the poor fish. He ripped and clawed and every few seconds looked around, as if he knew he was doing something wrong. When he was finished with the first one, he dived back in, snagged another, and continued with his dinner.

"Makes me sick every time I see it," Mr. Murray mumbled.

Theo had never lost a case in Animal Court, but as he watched Otto enthusiastically destroying the Murrays' school of koi, he had a feeling that this case might not end on a good note.

After Otto had gorged himself on three of the koi, he was full. He slinked away, moving much slower, and the video turned to black.

"Anything else, Mr. Murray?" Judge Yeck asked.

"Well, I guess not. I think it's only fair that Mr. Kerr pay me for the damages. Those fish cost about forty dollars each, and I've lost eighteen of them. More important, I want it stopped. It's his otter, and he should be required to keep the little monster away from my property. That's all I can think of, Judge."

"Any questions, Theo?"

"Sure, Your Honor." Theo looked at Mr. Murray and asked, "Where did you get the koi?"

"The Internet. There's an outfit in Miami that sells them. I think they come from Japan. You can buy them in most pet shops, but I get the high-end koi from a specialist who imports them."

"Out where you live do you ever see any raccoons or groundhogs?"

"Oh sure."

"How about cats, foxes, or herons?"

"I guess, from time to time, we see most everything. We're in the city limits, but it's kind of rural out there."

"Would you agree that these predators can also empty a goldfish pond?"

"You just saw the video, son. That wasn't a raccoon or a fox. I know the difference."

"Thank you. That's all I have, Judge."

"Call your first witness."

"Mr. John Kerr."

"Okay, Mr. Kerr, keep your seat and raise your right hand. Do you swear to tell the truth?"

"I do."

"Continue, Theo."

Theo held a yellow legal pad, just like a real lawyer. He'd managed to scribble some notes, handwriting he could barely read. "Now, Mr. Kerr, tell us about Otto."

Mr. Kerr looked around nervously and thought for a second. "Well, we've had otters before, along with beavers, raccoons, skunks, foxes, cats, possums, you name it. We have two acres and two ponds and a lot thick woods, so just about everything shows up sooner or later. This one little guy, the kids call him Otto, started hanging around a couple of years ago, and he's very friendly, not afraid of humans like most wild animals. We feed him and take care of him. I even took him to the vet once when he got sick. But I wouldn't call him a pet. He's never stayed in the house or garage. He won't come when you call him, and he certainly is not house trained. Point is, I can't control what he does. He's a wild animal, and if he wants to raid someone's pond I can't stop him. I don't control his life."

"And that's him in the video?"

"Sure looks like him, but then most otters look the same, I guess. I don't know. I don't spend much time thinking about otters."

"Do you have a dog?"

"Sure, got two of them."

"And do you have permits for them?"

"Yes, the city requires it."

"Do you have a cat?"

"Yes."

"Do you have a permit for the cat?"

"Yes, as required."

"Do you have a permit for Otto?"

"Of course not. He's a wild animal. You can't get a permit for a wild animal, right, Judge?"

Judge Yeck replied, "That's correct."

Theo said, "No further questions, Your Honor, and Mr. Kerr is our only witness."

"Very well. Mr. Murray, do you have any questions for Mr. Kerr?"

"No, sir. He admitted it was his otter. That's all that matters."

"Anything else, Mr. Murray?"

"Can't think of anything, no, sir."

"Theo?"

"Yes, sir." Theo stood with his legal pad.

"You can keep your seat, Theo."

"I know, Your Honor, but I need to stretch my legs." In truth, Theo preferred to stand and perhaps pace a little, just like the great trial lawyers he'd watched over the years. In real court, the lawyers always stood when addressing the judge or the jury, or when they were questioning witnesses.

Judge Yeck nodded and smiled. Theo began: "Judge, it looks like we're dealing with the laws of the jungle here. What if a raccoon lived in a tree on the Kerr property, and one day discovered these beautiful fish in Mr. Murray's water garden? You can't blame the raccoon for doing what he's supposed to do—find food. And you can't blame Mr. Kerr for something the raccoon does. Same for foxes, cats, blue herons, beavers—the woods are full of predators. Same for otters. They've lived around here forever, I suppose. This is their natural habitat. They have the right to come and go as they please and eat whatever they can find. These koi, on the other hand, are not native to this area. They come all the way from Japan. Who belongs here? I guess all the animals do, but in nature some animals prey on others. We can't change that. They have to eat, don't they? What's Mr. Kerr supposed to do? Catch the otter and keep him in a cage? That's not natural. Otto would probably die."

"Let's hope so," Mr. Murray interrupted.

"Hang on," Judge Yeck said, frowning at Mr. Murray.

Theo kept going: "My point is, Your Honor, Otto is not a domestic pet. He sleeps in the wild, roams at night, and eats whatever he can find. My client has no control over what this animal does. And, Your Honor, I don't have to remind the court that it's not against the law for otters to eat fish wherever they can find them."

Theo sat down and Judge Yeck said, "Good point, Theo, but I'm really bothered by the video. The proof seems pretty clear."

"Can I shoot him, Judge?" Mr. Murray blurted.

"Who? Otto or Theo?"

"That damned otter. Oh, sorry. That stinking otter."

"No, you cannot. Discharging a firearm within the city limits is against the law."

"Okay, then can I poison him?"

Judge Yeck thought for a second and said, "Yes, you can. The law says you cannot kill a dog, cat, horse, pig, lamb, goat, deer, bear, eagle, hawk, or an owl. It says nothing about otters."

"Don't forget beavers," Theo added helpfully.

"Right, and for some reason, beavers."

"Good," Mr. Murray said smugly. "Then, if Mr. Kerr will not take care of the otter, I'll get some poison and handle things myself."

Judge Yeck looked at Mr. Kerr and asked, "Are you familiar with the Wildlife Center over in Waynesburg?"

"No, sir."

"It's a refuge for wild animals that have been caught or need to be restrained for some time. I've ordered several animals to be sent over there, and the folks do a good job. I suggest you take Otto there, let the staff keep him for a few weeks while they find a place to relocate him. Somewhere far away."

"I guess we could do that," Mr. Kerr said.

"What about my dead fish?" Mr. Murray asked. "That otter ate about twenty of them and they cost forty bucks each."

Theo said, "Well, Your Honor, the proof shows that Otto ate only three of the fish. There's no proof that he ate the others. Could've been a raccoon or a fox."

"I doubt it," Judge Yeck said. "On the video he looks like he knows exactly what he's doing. I'll reduce it a little, but I'm ordering your client to pay five hundred dollars in damages."

"That sounds like a lot," Mr. Kerr said.

"Well, keep in mind, Mr. Kerr, that I could send Animal Control out there tomorrow and have the otter caught and put to sleep."

Mr. Kerr fell silent, and Theo had nothing else to say. Mr. Murray shrugged as if he was okay with the ruling. Judge Yeck said, "So ordered. Five hundred in damages and take the otter to the Wildlife Center. Anything else? Good. Court's adjourned."

They filed out of the courtroom and walked outside. Theo followed Byron and Mr. Kerr to their truck. Sitting in the cab was Byron's older brother, Billy, and Otto, who was asleep behind the steering wheel.

Byron said, "Thanks, Theo, you did the best you could."

Mr. Kerr said, "Nice job, Theo. You're gonna make a fine lawyer someday. Do I owe you anything?"

"No, sir. I can't charge fees yet. I'm only thirteen."

"Thanks, son."

Theo watched them drive away. It wasn't a good win, but then it wasn't a bad loss either. Neither side was satisfied with the outcome, so, as Judge Gantry often said, justice prevailed.

21

The offices of Boone & Boone were usually deserted by six p.m. Elsa left every day at five on the dot, with few exceptions. Vince and Dorothy, the two paralegals, soon followed. Mr. Boone was known to ease out even earlier, often under the guise of "running by the courthouse," which everyone knew was an excuse to meet his buddies for a drink. Mrs. Boone was always the last to leave, but it was unusual for her to be there until six.

After leaving Animal Court, Theo rode his bike to the office and was surprised that everyone was still there. All the lights were on. A big meeting of some sort was taking place in the conference room. He tiptoed down the hallway and tried to eavesdrop through the door, but couldn't hear much. Elsa, Vince, and Dorothy were in the meeting, along with his parents, who never worked together on a case. Theo could not remember such a gathering. He went back to his office and finished his homework, most of which he'd completed during his extra study hall.

Vince tapped on his door and stepped in. "Say, Theo, your mother wants to see you in the conference room."

What have I done now, Theo wondered. "What's going on in there?" he asked.

"We're meeting with the five schoolteachers. They've hired the firm to represent them."

"All five?"

"Yep."

"That's unusual in a criminal case, isn't it?"

"Very. They plan to stick together while we try to get the charges dismissed. If that doesn't happen, then they'll be forced to hire separate lawyers."

"Okay. Why does my mother want me in the conference room?"

"I guess you'll have to find out."

"Am I in trouble?"

"Not that I'm aware of."

Theo followed Vince to the conference room, where everyone was sitting around the long table and waiting for him. His mother, in charge, of course, stood and said,

"Theo, our firm is representing these five teachers from East Middle School." She introduced each of the five. Theo just stood at one end of the table and nodded. This is weird, he thought. What am I doing here?

Mr. Paul London stood and said, "Theo, we have something we would like to say to you. We are completely to blame for this scandal, and we accept responsibility. We changed the test scores for a number of our eighth graders, and this enabled them to qualify for the Honors track next year at Strattenburg High. We had our reasons for doing so, but our reasons are not good enough. We offer no excuses. Our actions unfairly helped some of our students and unfairly harmed those at other schools. Including you. If we had not cheated on behalf of our kids, there is an excellent chance you would have made Honors. We feel terrible about this, and we offer you our sincere apology."

Theo thought the poor guy was going to cry. It was obvious he felt far worse about the cheating than Theo did. The other teachers were staring at him with sad, mournful eyes.

Theo had been taught to accept an apology as soon as it was offered. Shake hands. Forget about it, and move on. He said, "Sure, Mr. London, I accept your apology. I just hope you guys are not punished too severely."

"We'll survive. We have a good lawyer."

"I'm gonna be okay, too," Theo said. "Whatever happens. I just don't want to take those tests again." Everyone laughed, and the humor cut the tension. Theo was excused and walked back to his office.

Thursday dinner was always at the same Turkish café, usually at the same table. Omar owned the place and greeted them warmly each week. Menus were not needed because they had the same red pepper hummus with pita bread, followed by the same roasted chicken. Mr. Boone once made the mistake of having a cup of Omar's Turkish coffee with dessert, and he didn't sleep for three days. Now, they drank only water. Theo enjoyed the place but often grew tired of Omar's constant interruptions. While his son ran the kitchen, Omar worked the front and felt like it was his business to engage his customers with nonstop chatting. He was also known to eavesdrop on conversations.

In low voices, the Boones tried to talk about the cheating scandal, but Omar was lurking nearby. They changed subjects and tried to talk about Ike and his latest problem, but Omar was too close. So they talked about an upcoming camping trip Troop 1440 was planning.

Theo didn't mind the five days of extra study hall punishment handed down by Mrs. Gladwell, but the month of no golf was painful. On Saturday morning, he sat at the kitchen table and tried to look as pitiful as possible as his father went about his routine as if life was just perfect. The weather was gorgeous, the golf course was calling, and Theo couldn't play. Mr. Boone, however, was planning a marvelous outing with three of his buddies.

"Sorry you can't play today, Theo," his father said. "But when you skip school you have to take your punishment."

"Thanks, Dad. I thought we already had this conversation."

"Just wanted to remind you."

"I got the message."

"That's enough, Woods," Mrs. Boone said as she drank her coffee.

"It's such a beautiful day," Mr. Boone said. "We might play twenty-seven holes."

And I hope you double-bogey every one of them, Theo almost blurted. But he ate his Cheerios in silence, suffering as much as possible. Even triple-bogey.

After Mr. Boone finally left, his mother asked, "So what are your plans for today, Theo?"

"I need to go find April. She's not doing too well these days."

"What's the problem?"

"She needs some help."

"Oh, really. What's going on?"

He hated to break a promise, but he also needed his mother's advice. Theo told her about Janelle the babysitter, and her sister Binky, and the letter April had sent to Dr. Stoop. He told her everything.

Mrs. Boone listened with great interest, and when Theo finished she said, "Well, I'm not sure April should be blaming herself. From what I know at this point, it looks as though the scandal was going to be discovered anyway. The test results looked suspicious, and the school board was investigating."

"That's what I keep telling her."

"So you knew the names of two of the teachers from the beginning?"

"I guess. I knew what April told me. I'm not sure I believed her."

"Why didn't you tell me?"

"Because I promised April I would never tell. I can keep a secret, Mom, but sometimes when you're just a kid the secret gets too big and you need help. Right now I'm worried about April. Plus, you're a lawyer and you know how important it is to keep the secrets of your clients."

"April is not your client."

"She thinks she is."

"And you're not a lawyer."

"I know. I just didn't want to get in the middle of all this."

"She should not send the second letter, Theo. That will just make her life more complicated."

"I know. I've told her. But she can be very stubborn."

"I suggest you have another chat with April and make sure she does not send another letter."

"Okay. That's what I'll do. I didn't want to play golf anyway."

22

The Sunday newspaper ran a long article about the scandal and the problems it was causing. The criminal charges added a new layer of intrigue to the story, and the chance that the teachers might go to jail seemed to bother a lot of people. It certainly bothered their lawyer, and Mrs. Boone's photo was on page two. She declined to discuss the case with the reporter, saying it was her professional responsibility to stay quiet and fight the charges in court, not in the press. This was unusual, Theo thought. Nowadays it seemed as though lawyers couldn't wait to jump in front of cameras and chat with reporters. He admired his mother for staying out of the limelight. Dr. Carmen Stoop likewise had little to say. She took the position that the matter was now headed for court, and until things were resolved there she would stay quiet. Jack Hogan, the prosecutor, was notorious for saying little to the press, but based on the tone of the article, he was taking some heat for pursuing the teachers in criminal court.

Mrs. Boone had filed a thick motion demanding that the charges be dismissed. Judge Henry Gantry had decided to grant her wish for a speedy hearing and scheduled one for the following Thursday. Mrs. Boone had not mentioned the hearing to Theo, probably because she suspected he would immediately start scheming of ways to get into the courtroom.

And she was right. He started right then, on Sunday morning as he read the newspaper. He said nothing to his parents, but the wheels were already turning. How could he, Theo Boone, the only kid lawyer in Strattenburg, miss such an important event? It was unthinkable. He almost choked on his Cheerios when he hatched the idea that he could be considered one of the victims of the scandal; thus, he would need to be in the courtroom.

What a great idea.

Without complaining, he showered and dressed for church. He sat through the worship service with a smile on his face and didn't hear a word the pastor said. Over lunch with his parents, he chatted about his next debate and his next camping trip, never once mentioning the scandal or anything related to it. Sunday afternoon he met April at Guff's and finally convinced her not to send any more letters. One was enough.

First thing Monday morning, he cornered Mr. Mount after homeroom and laid out his plan. The hearing in Judge Gantry's courtroom would be the perfect place for another field trip, for Mr. Mount's class to observe the judicial process in action.

Mr. Mount was not so sure but said he'd think about it.

Late Monday afternoon, Theo stopped by Ike's office. Parked outside was a brand-new bicycle, a ten speed with a helmet strapped to the seat. Ike said, "They took away my car keys for six months so I'm biking it now. I need the exercise." He was drinking coffee from a paper cup and looked fresh, even bright-eyed.

"I've stopped drinking, Theo. No more booze for me. This DUI has taught me a valuable lesson, and I'm sobering up."

"That's great, Ike. I'm proud of you."

"Booze is a dead-end street, Theo. Don't ever start drinking, okay?"

"I've managed to avoid the stuff so far."

"You're only thirteen. Wait until you get to high school

and start driving. That's when the trouble starts. Promise me you'll say no when a buddy offers you the first beer."

Actually, that had already happened. Theo was hanging out at Woody's house one day when his parents were away. The refrigerator was full of beer, and Woody thought it would be cool to drink a few. Theo declined and left not long afterward.

"I promise, Ike," he said. "And I'm proud of you."

"You're one of the reasons, Theo, to be honest. I was humiliated when my favorite nephew came to the jail to rescue me. I finally realized that enough was enough, and I promised that I would never again put myself in a situation like that. I'm quitting for my own well-being, but I'm also quitting for you. I want to set a better example."

His voice cracked a little, and his eyes moistened. Theo was not sure what to say.

Theo began his letter that night when he was supposed to be reading a book for English. The first draft began:

Dear Mrs. Gladwell:

As you probably know, Judge Henry Gantry has scheduled a big hearing this

Thursday at nine a.m. in his courtroom. The five schoolteachers from East Middle School have been charged with conspiracy and fraud, and, if convicted, might be sentenced to jail. Their lawyer, at least for this hearing, is my mother, Marcella Boone.

I feel as though I have the right to be in the courtroom to watch this important event. Please allow me to explain why.

As you know, I plan to become a lawyer when I grow up. I've spent many hours in courtrooms, especially Judge Gantry's, and I've watched many trials. I know all the judges and clerks, and many of the lawyers and policemen. When my friends are playing soccer or baseball, or off at summer camp, I'm usually hanging around the courthouse waiting for a trial to start. I've been doing this for years and I enjoy it a lot. It's not only entertaining but very educational. I see lawyers do things all the time that I know they shouldn't do, and there's nothing more

interesting, at least to me, than to watch a
trial with two great lawyers doing battle.
I love their final arguments when they try
to persuade the jury to see things their
way. And, there's nothing more tense and
dramatic than waiting for a jury to return
with its verdict.

You have been kind enough before to allow
Mr. Mount to take us on field trips to the
courthouse to watch trials and talk to judges.
The hearing this Thursday will be the perfect
time to take another field trip.

Over dinner tonight I discussed this
with my parents. They feel as though I
should spend the day in class and not in the
courtroom. I'm still working on them, but
things do not look too good on that front.

There's another reason I should be in the
courtroom. The five teachers are charged with
committing crimes, though, personally, I think
this is wrong. Anyway, a crime means there is

a victim, and the victim is always expected to be in court. I've seen many victims testify and point fingers at the defendants. I've seen many victims sit in the front row for days as the witnesses tell their stories.

In this case, the teachers are accused of cheating, and there is a good chance their cheating harmed a group of eighth graders who failed to score high enough on the standardized tests to make Honors. Some of us at Strattenburg Middle, and others at Central Middle, were probably excluded from the Honors program because of the cheating. At this point we don't know this for a fact, but it looks likely.

I don't know the names of the other students who are in the same boat with me. And I assume that most of them have no interest in watching the hearing. But, since I'm sort of a victim, I think it's important to attend the hearing. Also, since my mother is so involved, there is probably no other victim

who knows as much about the case. In fact, I
know a lot of things I shouldn't know.

There's another reason that you probably
won't care about. If I am forced to attend
class on Thursday, and miss this important
hearing, then I will be completely useless at
school. The day will be a waste for me because
my mind will be in the courtroom.

I realize you're probably still ticked off at
me for skipping school the other day and I'm
still very sorry about that. I promise it will
never happen again.

Please, Mrs. Gladwell, please allow Mr.
Mount's class to take another field trip and
watch the hearing on Thursday.

Sincerely,
Theo Boone

The more he wrote the better it sounded, and at midnight
he was still pecking away on his laptop. The "victim"

angle was pure genius, he thought, and he finally fell asleep filled with confidence that Mrs. Gladwell could not say no.

He wrote the final draft early Tuesday morning, printed it, and folded it into an envelope. He did not mention it to his parents. When he arrived at school, he took it straight to Mrs. Gladwell's office. He bypassed Miss Gloria because she would ask a dozen questions, and he placed the letter in the center of Mrs. Gladwell's desk.

During lunch, Mr. Mount found him in the cafeteria and handed him a small envelope. He tore it open and pulled out a handwritten note from Mrs. Gladwell. It read:

> *Dear Theo: Thanks for the letter but the answer is no. DG.*

Tuesday, after school, Theo and Judge climbed the stairs at Boone & Boone and walked into his father's office. Mr. Boone was hard at work with a pile of paperwork, his unlit pipe stuck in one corner of his mouth.

"How was school?" he asked.

"Boring. I can't concentrate these days, not with the big hearing coming up on Thursday and being kicked out of the courtroom and all. It just seems so unfair."

"Haven't we had this conversation?"

"I wouldn't call it a conversation. I've brought up the subject a couple of times and you guys just slam the door. I don't get to say much."

"Maybe there's not much to discuss. You're not missing school to go to court. It's really quite simple."

"I plan to boycott my classes on Thursday."

"I beg your pardon?"

"I'm boycotting. Not skipping. I'll be in class all right, but I will not listen to the teachers and I will not take part in any discussion. I'll do the homework because I'll get in trouble if I don't do the homework, but I plan to zone out and just sit there ignoring everything."

"And you call this a boycott?"

"Something like that. I can't think of a better word."

"Sounds pretty stupid to me. Just sitting in class like an imbecile while the world goes by."

"I don't care. I'm taking a stand. You guys won't let me go to court. I have to do something to protest."

"Protest all you want, but if you make bad grades you'll pay a price."

"I've got straight A's, Dad. One day of boycotting won't hurt my grades."

"Whatever. Don't you have Scouts today, or are you boycotting that, too?"

"I'm leaving now."

23

Wednesday afternoon, the five schoolteachers arrived at Boone & Boone for a big meeting. They gathered in the conference room with Mr. and Mrs. Boone, along with Vince and Dorothy. Elsa stayed at the front desk to answer the phone and do her work, and Theo watched and listened as much as possible, but heard nothing. "I think you'd better stay in your little room," Elsa warned him, and he retreated, again in defeat.

He had one last trick up his sleeve. A few minutes before five, he hopped on his bike and rode to the courthouse. Judge Gantry's courtroom was empty, just as Theo hoped. He walked down the hall to his office and said hello to Mrs. Hardy. She was arranging things on her desk and getting ready to leave.

"Is the judge in?" Theo asked.

"Yes, but he's very busy."

"I just need a minute."

"I'll see what I can do."

Five minutes later, Theo walked into Judge Gantry's large office. "Well, hello, Theo," the judge said. "What brings you here?"

"I need a favor," Theo said somewhat nervously.

"What a surprise. I'm sure it has something to do with the hearing tomorrow. Let me guess—you believe that we cannot properly conduct matters unless you're present in the courtroom. Right?"

"Something like that. Just curious, Judge, how long do you think it will last?"

"Couple of hours. It's not a trial, you know, just a hearing with a few witnesses and the attorneys arguing back and forth."

"And what time will you start?"

"It's scheduled for nine a.m., but there are a couple of matters on the docket before it. Some routine motions and such that shouldn't take too long. Why do you ask?"

"Well, Judge, as you know I spend a lot of time in the courtroom, more than any other kid I know, and it's not unusual for things to get delayed. Lawyers show up late, or the police, or the bailiffs can't get the people over from the jail on time. Or some lawyer doesn't have his paperwork in order, or a fifteen-minute hearing runs for an hour or more. Anyway, as you well know, there are a lot of reasons for things to run behind schedule."

"I run a pretty tight ship, Theo, if I do say so myself."

"Yes, sir, I know that, and I've watched other judges who are not as organized as you. But, still, things do get delayed, you know."

"Oh, I see. You want me to slow everything down in the morning."

"Well, what I had in mind was more like moving the hearing back to one or two in the afternoon, then sort of stalling until school is out."

"That's asking a lot, Theo."

"Yes, sir, I know, but I'm pretty desperate right now. Nothing else has worked. I've tried to explain to my parents and to my principal that since I have an interest in this case that I should be allowed to at least know what's going on."

"An interest in the case?"

"Yes, sir. I think I'm one of the victims."

"I don't follow."

"You see, Judge, I barely missed Honors, and it was probably because of the cheating at East Middle School."

"I didn't know that."

"It's not something we talk about, and, as far as I know, the names of the students who didn't make it have not been made public. In fact, the names and scores are kept confidential."

"I see. And what do your parents think about your being a victim?"

"I'm not sure they see my point. They certainly have not agreed to let me miss school and watch the hearing. I played hooky a couple of weeks ago, and they're still pretty sore about that. But I make straight A's, usually, and school is boring anyway. I think I'm ready for law school, to be honest."

Judge Gantry took a deep breath and rubbed his eyes. He stood and stretched and seemed very tired. He paced around his desk a few times, scratching his chin, deep in thought. Theo watched and waited, somewhat surprised that he'd gotten this far with his scheme. It was a long shot, and he fully expected the judge to order him out of his office with stern instructions to mind his own business. He, Judge Henry Gantry, did not need the help of a thirteen-year-old in managing his courtroom.

"You know, Theo, I'm inclined to agree with you."

"You are?" Theo blurted, stunned.

"Yes, I see your point, and it's a good one. You and the

other students who are in the same boat should be able to watch the hearing and see what happens."

"Really? I mean, sure, Judge. I agree."

Judge Gantry stepped to his desk, pressed a button on the intercom, and said, "Mrs. Hardy, would you please step in here?" He returned to his seat at the conference table and asked, "What time is school dismissed tomorrow?"

"Final bell is at three thirty, but my last period is a study hall that's easy to get out of. I could be here around two thirty I think."

"I wouldn't want to start later than that."

"Fine with me."

Mrs. Hardy walked in and Judge Gantry said to her, "I've reviewed my docket for tomorrow, and I'm afraid the first few matters might run a bit longer than expected. I'm resetting the motion to dismiss for two thirty. Please call the offices of Jack Hogan and Mrs. Boone, then follow up with e-mails."

"Certainly," she said, looking at Theo and wanting to ask, "What have you done now?" But she left, and when the door was closed, Judge Gantry said, "It's no big deal, really. These types of hearings get moved around all the time."

"It's your courtroom, right?" Theo asked.

"For now, anyway."

"Thanks."

"Run along now, and I'll see you tomorrow. And, Theo, not a word of this to anyone. The courtroom is open to the public, and if the other students wish to attend, so be it. But let's not advertise this, okay?"

Theo jumped to his feet and said, "Sure, Judge. See you tomorrow." As he grabbed the doorknob he turned and said, "Say, Judge, you really don't think they're criminals, do you?"

"That's enough, Theo. See you tomorrow."

24

Dinner was quiet. The Boones ate Chinese take-out in the den, and no one seemed interested in talking, which was unusual. Mr. and Mrs. Boone were thinking about the hearing tomorrow. Neither did much in the field of criminal law, and Theo sensed an uneasiness on their part. Mrs. Boone spent a lot of time in court, but almost always with divorce clients. Mr. Boone appeared before judges only once or twice a year. Theo was waiting for the right moment to bring up the subject of him missing study hall and hustling over to the courthouse at 2:30 to sit and watch it all. But, it was impossible to mention this when no one was talking. It had to be discussed, though, because Theo knew it was a bad idea to just show up without telling his parents why.

His first challenge would be to convince Mr. Mount that he was needed in court at 2:30, but he wasn't too worried about that.

Finally, he said, "Why is everyone so quiet?"

His mother said, "Oh, sorry, Theo, I was just thinking about something else."

Mr. Boone said, "I was just eating."

"Well, don't we always talk and eat at the same time?"

"Sure," his mother said. "What do you want to talk about?"

"Well, we could talk about the conflict in the Middle East or that typhoon in the Philippines, but that's not what you're thinking about. I suspect you're both worrying about tomorrow and the five clients that might be facing criminal trials and possibly going to jail. Right?"

Both of his parents smiled. His mother said, "Judge Gantry moved the hearing back to two thirty."

"Oh really? Wonder why he did that."

"It's not that unusual. He's a very busy judge with a crowded docket. I suppose you'll hurry over after school and watch things."

"If that's okay?"

"I'm not so sure about that," his father said. "It might not be a good idea for you to be in the courtroom."

"The courtroom is open to the public, Dad. There will be

a lot of people there—family members, school folks, reporters, maybe even some parents of eighth graders. It doesn't seem fair to keep me away."

"He's right, Woods," Mrs. Boone said. "There's nothing private about the hearing. It will be splashed all over the newspaper Friday morning."

"I agree," Theo said. "So it's okay if I show up?"

Both parents took a bite of rice at the exact same moment. His mother sort of nodded okay. His father sort of didn't, but Theo knew he was home free.

When the 8:40 bell rang for homeroom, Theo had been talking to Mr. Mount for the past ten minutes. Mr. Mount said, "I don't know, Theo. If I excuse you from study hall I'll have to inform Mrs. Gladwell. Any student leaving early must check out at the front office, you know that. She might still be a bit ticked off because you skipped a few days ago."

"She's always ticked off about something. That's her job."

"I don't know."

"Look, Mr. Mount, I had a chat with Judge Gantry yesterday in his office, and he thinks it's important for me to be in the courtroom."

"Seriously?"

"I wouldn't lie to you. In fact, and you can't tell anyone

this, but it was my idea to postpone the hearing for a few hours. You know how it is in court—stuff is always getting delayed and postponed. He has a few matters first thing in the morning, and I sort of convinced him to bump the hearing to the afternoon so I can be there. He wants me there, Mr. Mount. I can send him an e-mail if you'd like."

"No, no that's okay. I'll send a note to Mrs. Gladwell."

"Thanks."

By lunchtime, April was complaining of an upset stomach and seemed deathly ill. She called her mother who promptly called Miss Gloria and arranged for her to leave school as soon as possible.

When the bell rang at 2:20, Theo sprinted to his bike and sped off to court.

25

Judge Gantry was settling himself on his perch at the bench when Theo and April eased into the balcony and took two seats in the front row. Looking down, they had a perfect view and could see everything but the very back of the courtroom. To the left, beyond the bar, was the defense table, crowded with the five teachers and Mr. and Mrs. Boone. To the right was the prosecution's table where Mr. Jack Hogan and one of his assistants were seated. There was a nice crowd scattered throughout the spectators' seats. Theo figured those watching were friends and families of the teachers, along with some reporters and school personnel. He recognized a few lawyers, a few of the same ones who were always hanging around the courtroom when something interesting took place.

Judge Gantry began properly with, "Good afternoon. We are here on a motion by the defendants to dismiss the charges of fraud and conspiracy filed against them. Let the record reflect that all five are here, along with their attorneys of record, the Honorable Marcella Boone and the Honorable Woods Boone."

Theo often wondered why judges and lawyers insisted on referring to one another as "Honorable," but he had never found a satisfactory answer. Ike scoffed at this practice, said it was because no one else considered them to be so honorable.

Judge Gantry said, "Mrs. Boone, as lead counsel, you have filed this motion, so you have the burden going forward. How many witnesses do you have?"

Mrs. Boone stood and replied, "Six or seven."

"You may proceed."

"The defense calls Dr. Carmen Stoop to the stand, Your Honor."

Dr. Stoop rose from the front row, walked through the gate in the bar, and stopped at the witness stand where she raised her right hand and swore to tell the truth. When she was seated, she pulled the microphone a bit closer to her mouth and smiled at Mrs. Boone. She gave her name, address, and said she was the Superintendent of the Strattenburg City School District, a job she had held for the past eight years.

Dr. Stoop was highly regarded and commanded respect. The city was proud of its school system, and she got most of the credit for its success.

Mrs. Boone walked her through a series of questions about the standardized tests: the reasons behind them; how long they had been in place; changes that had been made; challenges they posed; problems they had created. Dr. Stoop admitted that she was not convinced the tests were the best method to measure the academic progress of the students. She admitted, frankly, that she preferred other methods, but the state had passed a law requiring the tests. The tests were tied to state funding, and if Strattenburg declined to partici- pate, which it had the option to do, then it would lose a lot of money. Limiting the discussion to the eighth grade, she described the results for the three middle schools over the past five years. East Middle had always lagged behind the other two, and this had been a major concern of the school board. Yes, the teachers at East were put under pressure to improve the scores or the school would face penalties.

Dr. Stoop was a veteran who was smart and calm. She knew what she was talking about and was quite candid. Theo and April watched and listened with rapt atten- tion. Theo was especially proud of his mother. She moved around the courtroom in complete control and with total confidence. He had never seen her in a courtroom before, primarily because in most of her cases the courtrooms were closed to the public.

She asked about the most recent round of tests, and Dr. Stoop explained that the results were good overall, top ten percent in the state, with the exception of East Middle. However, even there, the scores showed an impressive improvement.

"Did the rise in scores at East raise any suspicions in your office?" Mrs. Boone asked.

"Not at first. We were thrilled with the results when we first saw them, but after looking closer we began to have a few doubts. We decided to look into some of the individual test results."

"What did you find?"

"A higher number of erasures. A lot of the eighth graders seemed to have chosen the wrong answers initially, then, after erasing them, somehow managed to pick the right answer every time."

"Can you give us an example?"

"Yes. At your request, I brought a couple of the test results. I believe you have them."

Mrs. Boone walked to her table and reached for a file. She handed copies to Jack Hogan, Judge Gantry, and to the witness. Dr. Stoop explained that the first document was the score sheet for an unnamed East eighth grader, and it showed the answers for twenty math questions. The student at first missed half of the problems, then he or she erased seven of the original answers and recorded the correct ones. "Seven for seven was a red flag," Dr. Stoop said. As the red flags piled up, she and her staff began to realize they might have a problem.

"How many eighth graders were tested at East Middle School?" Mrs. Boone asked.

"One hundred and eighteen. We began checking all of them, and the problem was unfolding when I received the anonymous letter. It came from a 'concerned citizen' and it really upset everyone. It was specific and mentioned the names of two eighth-grade teachers who allegedly changed scores."

April reached for Theo's hand and squeezed it until he could almost feel bones crunching.

Mrs. Boone handed copies of the letter to Jack Hogan and Judge Gantry, then asked Dr. Stoop to read it aloud. When she did, April flinched and seemed to hold her breath.

When she finished, Mrs. Boone asked, "What was your reaction to the letter?"

"Well, we were stunned, to say the least. I met with our

school board attorney, Mr. Robert McNile, and we decided to immediately conduct a thorough investigation, one that led us to the five teachers."

"Nothing more at this time, Your Honor."

Judge Gantry looked at the prosecutor and said, "Mr. Hogan?"

Jack Hogan stood, walked to the podium, and politely said, "Thank you, Dr. Stoop. Now, I would like you to explain the bonus system that applies to some of your teachers."

"Certainly. It's not a good system and not one that I favor, though we really have no choice. It was implemented by the state, and we have no say in the matter. Basically, it provides for merit-based pay increases of up to five thousand dollars for teachers whose students improve dramatically on the the standardized tests."

"What's considered a dramatic improvement?"

"There is a formula that is hopelessly complicated, but, generally speaking, if the entire eighth grade shows an overall improvement rate of fifteen percent from the previous year, and fifteen percent of the class lands in the top ten percent for the city, then the teachers qualify for a bonus. Other factors include the teacher's experience and number of college degrees. Again, I don't like the bonus scheme.

All of our teachers are underpaid, and it seems silly to reward one small group."

"Would you agree that these five teachers had a financial reason to change test scores?"

"Frankly, Mr. Hogan, I cannot speculate as to their reasons."

"Thank you, Dr. Stoop. Nothing further at this time, Your Honor."

"You are excused, Dr. Stoop," Judge Gantry said. "Call your next witness."

Mrs. Boone stood and said, "Mr. Paul London."

Theo knew his parents were taking a chance. They planned to put all five defendants on the witness stand and have them discuss their roles in the scandal. In doing so, the teachers would admit to doing things that were wrong. They would say that they deserved to be punished, but the punishment should not come from the criminal justice system; rather, it should come from the school board. They would be fired as teachers. Their professional careers would be over; their reputations damaged; their lives seriously damaged if not ruined. They would probably never teach again. But, they did not deserve to be tried, convicted, and labeled as felons. By being completely honest about what they had done, perhaps in the end they might win favor with the judge.

Paul London was an impressive witness. He had taught for twenty years and won every award the city offered. He loved the classroom and his students loved him. He had a master's degree and for the past ten years had been working on his doctorate. He took full responsibility for changing the test scores. He had recruited the other four teachers to join him; it was all his fault.

Why? Well, it had begun a few years back when he grew tired of seeing his students fall short on the standardized tests. He changed a few scores to help his students, then a few more. Many of the kids at East, his kids, were from lower income families, and they didn't have the same opportunities as other students at other schools. It was frustrating to watch them fall short on the standardized tests that were unfair to begin with—and be labeled slow learners.

When Mr. London described his students, he did so with great compassion, and eloquence. His testimony became a dramatic performance, one that captivated the courtroom. He looked at Judge Gantry and said, "How can you compare a student with only one parent who lives in a tiny apartment with a student with two parents and grandparents and private tutors when necessary? How can you compare a student whose parents speak little or no English to a student whose parents have college degrees?

How can you compare a student whose father is in prison to a student whose father is a doctor? How can you compare a student who had nothing for breakfast with a student who ate too much for breakfast? How can you compare a student who started preschool as a three-year-old to a student who arrived here too late for kindergarten?"

The courtroom was still and silent. Judge Gantry nodded and said nothing. No response was expected.

Mr. London sneered at the idea that the teachers were cheating for extra money. He said, "My salary now is almost fifty thousand a year, after twenty years in the classroom, and I'm expected to spend a chunk of that buying supplies for my students. I even buy food for them. A few extra bucks in bonus money is not going to help me or the other teachers. That's a ridiculous accusation. We never thought about the money. We were just trying to help our kids. That's all."

When Mrs. Boone sat down, Jack Hogan rose and asked, "So you admit to changing test scores?"

"I do."

"And you admit to doing this with the other four teachers?"

"I do."

"And you admit to knowing there was the possibility of financial gain for you and the others?"

"I do, yes, sir."

"I have nothing else at this time, Your Honor."

A conspiracy was a group effort to do something wrong, and Theo realized that Paul London had just admitted, under oath, to being part of a conspiracy. The question would be: Was the "wrong" they conspired to do really a crime? If Judge Gantry believed their efforts were driven by a desire to collect bonuses, then they would be treated like criminal defendants.

After Paul London's performance, Theo doubted anyone could really believe the teachers' motives were driven by money.

The next witness was Emily Novak, a twelve-year veteran at East Middle School and one of the two April had named in her letter. Not long after she stated her name and address, she broke down and started crying. She pulled herself together, but for the next fifteen minutes was on the verge of more tears. One of her favorite students was a young girl from a bad home, a place where she was always in danger. She had been mistreated by various relatives and abandoned by her mother. She felt safe at school and considered the teachers to be her protectors. For the girl, school was more about physical safety and a stable environment—in other words, survival. Learning was not as important. She fell behind in every class, and Ms. Novak spent hours with her trying to catch up. When the tests were given, the girl had just been placed in a different foster home. Not surprisingly, her scores were terrible. Ms. Novak altered some of her answers, but the girl was still placed in Remedial. She quit school halfway through the ninth grade and disappeared. Ms. Novak considered herself a failure for not doing more to save the girl, but at least she tried. There was no excuse for changing her scores, but it was important to look at the scandal from the view of the teachers.

When she started crying again, Theo looked at April. She had tears in her eyes, and she was shaking her head. She whispered, "I feel perfectly rotten, Theo."

Two hours passed quickly as they listened to the five teachers admit their wrongdoing and give their reasons. At 4:30, Judge Gantry called for a fifteen-minute recess. Theo and April stayed in their seats. "What do you think, Theo?" she asked quietly.

"I don't know but I'm worried. All five have admitted their guilt, so there's no way they will ever go to trial. If Judge Gantry allows the criminal charges to stand, then the best they can hope for is some kind of plea bargain."

"What does that mean?"

"It means they'll plead guilty in return for a light sentence."

"But they'll still go to jail?"

"Not always. For crimes that are not that serious, ones

that do not involve violence or large amounts of money or defendants with bad records, they sometimes work out a deal where they are required to pay a fine and put on probation for a few years. If they screw up again, then they go to jail. But they will always have a criminal record."

"They seem like such good teachers."

"Yes, they do."

When the courtroom was settled, Mrs. Boone walked to the podium and began: "Your Honor, we've heard the honest and sincere testimony from these five defendants. They have all admitted wrongdoing. They are remorseful beyond words. They are professional educators who allowed their emotions to lead them into bad decisions. They have already been punished by being suspended from the classroom, by facing the likelihood of losing their jobs, and by the damage to their careers and reputations. What good is more punishment? What good comes from allowing these five excellent teachers to be chewed up by our criminal justice system? If you allow these charges to go forward, each of the five will be forced to hire lawyers, at great expense, with money they don't have. Each will face the humiliation of a trial and more public attention. Each will run the risk of going to jail. Jails and prisons are for criminals, Your Honor, not for schoolteachers."

She paused and walked to the edge of the jury box, though it was empty. She spoke without notes but with great conviction. Theo had watched many fine lawyers in court, and at that moment his mother was one of the best. He felt enormous pride and was surprised to realize that his throat felt tight. Was he getting choked up? He swallowed hard.

"Now, the claim by the prosecution that these teachers entered into a conspiracy to commit fraud for financial gain is ridiculous. You heard their words, Your Honor. They were not motivated by money. They did not risk their careers over a few bucks in bonus money. What they did was wrong, but what they did had only one goal and that was to help their students survive in this super-competitive environment that we have created. We, Judge, all of us. We expect the best for our children, and we allow the school system to classify them so that the brighter ones will be rewarded even further. It's a bad system, Judge, and one that we should do away with. I know—that's not my role in all of this. But, it helps to explain what they did."

She walked to the defense table and waved her hand at the five. "My clients did not engage in criminal behavior, Your Honor, and I demand that these charges be dismissed." When she sat down, the courtroom was silent.

Jack Hogan stood slowly and walked to the podium. He

was an old pro Theo had watched many times. He said,
"Thank you, Your Honor. When I was in the sixth grade,
a long time ago, my favorite teacher was Mrs. Greenwood.
She was funny, smart, pretty, and she was strict. She taught
history and she gave really hard tests, so hard that I was
having trouble in the class. One day we were taking a final
exam, a really long, difficult test, and three of us figured
out a way to cheat. It was multiple choice, and I was sitting
right behind the smartest kid in class. He agreed to move
his paper to the far side of his desk so I could peek over his
shoulder. Once I stole the correct answers, I signaled them
to my other two buddies. It worked brilliantly until we were
caught. Mrs. Greenwood got suspicious, confiscated our
exams, and marched us down to the principal's office. Since
all three of us had the same answers there wasn't much we
could say. My father had taught me the dangers of lying, so
I admitted to cheating. I told the truth. It was a bad scene.
My two buddies and I were suspended for a week and put
on probation. I was embarrassed and never felt tempted to
cheat again. Mrs. Greenwood was very disappointed, and I
was crushed by this. What did we learn? Well, we learned a
valuable lesson in what was right and what was wrong. We
learned that cheating was wrong and led to bad results. And
we were the kids, the students. I could never imagine Mrs.

Greenwood cheating, or any of my other teachers for that matter. Students sometimes cheat, but not teachers! They make and enforce the rules. They teach right from wrong. They set a proper example. They are the adults in charge of our children, and when they cheat and cover up it's far worse than when the students do it.

"Your Honor, we now know that these five people knowingly, and intentionally, and even with the expectation of one day getting caught, entered into a conspiracy to provide fraudulent test results. That's a crime in my book! They scoff at the idea that it was for money, but money was a potential factor. This cannot be denied. They don't make much money so maybe they wanted some more. I don't know, but if we are allowed to go forward with these charges then we'll learn everything. It's premature at this point to say, oh well, let's just let the school board deal with it. No, sir, that's letting them off too easy. My office brought these charges, and we are prepared to fully prosecute them. Thank you."

Jack Hogan sat down and everyone took a deep breath. Judge Gantry finally asked, "Anything else?"

The lawyers shook their heads. No.

"All right. I want to sleep on this, and I'll issue a ruling by noon tomorrow. Court's adjourned."

26

As Theo and April were leaving the balcony, a bailiff stopped them at the door and said, "Say, Theo, Judge Gantry wants you to stop by his office."

Theo was startled. "Okay, when?"

"Right now."

"Sure." He said good-bye to April and hurried away, dodging the spectators as they filed out of the main courtroom. Judge Gantry was waiting with his door opened. He closed it when Theo walked in. He removed his black robe, said, "Have a seat," and pointed to a chair at the conference table. Theo did as he was instructed. Judge Gantry sat down and loosened his tie. He gave Theo a hard look and asked, "What do you think?"

Theo wasn't sure what the judge wanted so he just shrugged, as if confused.

"You know, Theo, we often make the law too complicated. We take a set of facts and analyze them ten different
ways and try to figure out what laws should apply and how
and why, when, in reality, a lot of cases are pretty simple.
Simple enough for a young person to see clearly, when we
try so hard to make them confusing. Does this make sense?"

"I think so."

"I'd like to know how you would rule in this case, Theo.
You're thirteen years old, a smart kid who knows more law
than most lawyers, and also someone who's sort of involved
in this mess. What would you do, after hearing what we've
just heard?"

Man up, Theo told himself. He's talking to you like
an adult, so act like one. "They're not criminals, Judge.
What they did was really bad. I mean the idea of a bunch
of teachers hiding in a room erasing wrong answers and
loading up with the correct ones is pretty outrageous. I
understand why they did it, but it was still a rotten thing
to do. Like Jack Hogan said, they're supposed to teach us
right from wrong."

"Agreed. It's disgusting."

"But they will be punished enough. They're good people
who did something wrong, but what they did was not a
crime. I would dismiss the charges, Judge."

"You like secrets don't you, Theo?"

"Love 'em."

"Good. Here's a secret you can't talk about until noon tomorrow. I'm dismissing the charges. Right now it's just between you and me." He reached out a hand and Theo shook it.

"A secret, right?"

"You got it, Judge."

The Boones enjoyed dinner with Omar in his café, and when he wasn't around his parents talked nonstop about the hearing. Mrs. Boone was relieved and relaxed, and Theo congratulated her on a fine performance. Mr. Boone was happy to play second fiddle to his wife, and it was obvious he was very proud.

"You should do more trial work, Mom. You're very much at home in the courtroom."

"Thank you, Teddy, but I have enough work to keep me busy."

"Things could not have gone better, dear," Mr. Boone said. "You were superb."

"I'll feel superb when we win," she said. Theo bit his tongue. He was often tempted to unload secrets on his parents, but not this time. He was determined to prove he could be trusted. Instead he said, "I watched Judge Gantry a lot, and I think he is with the teachers. Don't you agree, Dad?"

"No doubt about it. He'll dismiss the charges and we can move on."

"Let's not get too confident," Mrs. Boone said. "When I'm sure I've won, something bad usually happens, and when I know I've lost, there is usually a pleasant surprise. It's a tricky business trying to predict what a judge will do."

Theo kept a mouth full of food and tried to say as little as possible.

Late that night he called April, and they chatted for almost an hour about the courtroom drama. She had been scared out of her mind when Dr. Stoop read her letter and almost fainted. But now that she was able to look back, she didn't feel so bad about sending it. The letter had prompted the school officials to take the matter seriously and investigate immediately.

"Aren't you glad you didn't send that second letter?" Theo asked. "Otherwise you might have been on the witness stand today."

"I sure am. Thank you, Theo. I had made up my mind to send it, but you talked me out of it."

"Always trust your lawyer, April."

27

The Friday morning newspaper had the story on the front page, complete with a great front-page photo of Mr. and Mrs. Boone walking into the courtroom, each holding a thick briefcase and looking like they were ready for business. It was a lawyer's dream. A long story described the hearing. There were summaries of the testimony and arguments from the lawyers.

Theo read it quickly and hurried off to school. The morning passed slowly.

At three minutes before noon, Judge Gantry posted online a two-page ruling dismissing the criminal charges against the teachers. He said, in part, "While I am disturbed by the actions of the defendants, their behavior did not rise to the level of criminal activity."

Theo texted congratulations to his parents and went to the cafeteria for lunch.

At two p.m., Dr. Carmen Stoop issued a statement to the press. She announced that the school board had no choice but to terminate the contracts of the five teachers. Two years from now they would be allowed to reapply for teaching positions in the school system.

This surprised no one; but what followed did. Dr. Stoop said that the results from the previous testing would be disregarded at all grade levels. And, furthermore, the Strattenburg School District would no longer participate in the standardized tests required by the state. The district could "opt out" of the testing, but doing so would mean the loss of significant state funding.

In her statement, she said, "This city has always placed a priority on good schools and providing the best education possible for our students. We will continue to do so. This will require a lot of community support and more money from our city council. Frankly, we believe we are in a better position to educate our children than the people at the state level. To do so will take a great effort from all of our citizens."

Theo read the statement online and couldn't suppress a

smile. No more standardized testing. No more "teaching to the tests." No more tracking. No more competition for the Honors track. No more special classes for gifted students and lesser classes for lesser students.

He went to find April.

Elsa put together the party with little effort. She called a deli and it delivered a tray of finger sandwiches, another of brownies and cookies, two gallons of punch, and three bottles of champagne. She called the defendants and invited them to stop by for a small celebration.

Theo knew that every schoolteacher was starving by late afternoon. They were on their feet all day with little time to eat. The offer of good food and something to drink was irresistible. By 4:30 Friday, all five of the former East Middle School teachers were in the conference room—four with their spouses. Geneva Hull brought her current boyfriend. Every member of the Boone law firm was there.

Though their futures were unknown, and certainly not promising, they were in the mood to celebrate, if only for a short time. They were no longer considered criminals and would not face the nightmare of being prosecuted. For hard-working educators who had little or no dealings with the criminal justice system, the prospect of going to jail had been terrifying. Now that had passed. They could pick up the pieces and try to get on with their lives. For a short time that Friday afternoon, they were happy and wanted to unwind. They also wanted to thank their lawyers.

Theo and April sat in a corner and sipped punch. They were relieved, too. The scandal was finally over, and they could talk about something else.

THEODORE BOONE:
THE FUGITIVE

HE WAS SUPPOSED TO BE HAVING FUN WITH HIS FRIENDS, NOT PLAYING DETECTIVE AND STALKING A SERIAL KILLER.

THEODORE BOONE – teenage lawyer and courtroom hero – is on a class trip seeing the sights of the capital city. But he hadn't counted on seeing the most wanted man in the history of his home town, Strattenburg.

Suddenly Theo is caught in the hunt for an accused murderer, alongside the FBI. Theo knows he's getting in deep – and things could become even more dangerous. Because if this case goes back to court, it will be down to him to testify.

Will justice finally be done, or will the killer's criminal allies be out for revenge?

THEODORE BOONE:
THE ACTIVIST

'HOW ABOUT IT, THEO?', SEBASTIAN SAID.

'THEY'VE ALREADY TRIED TO KILL YOUR DOG.'

THEODORE BOONE's town is under threat, from a group of corrupt men planning to build a freeway bypass and destroy countless homes.

Now thirteen-year-old Theo – the schoolboy lawyer destined for the courtroom – must stand up for his city and stop them. But soon the fight turns nasty, and Theo and his friends face a giant battle against the underhand crooks.

And when Theodore uncovers a terrible secret – a secret he's discovered illegally – he is torn.

Should Theo stop the shady developers from breaking the law by breaking it himself?

THEODORE BOONE:
THE ACCUSED

'BELIEVE ME, HE'S CONVINCED I'M GUILTY
AND HE'S OUT FOR BLOOD.'

THEODORE BOONE is obsessed with the courtroom,
justice and prosecuting the guilty. But now thirteen-
year-old Theo stands accused.

Stolen property has been found in his locker and
soon Theo is under investigation. Somebody is
sabotaging his reputation and framing him as a
criminal.

As the evidence against him mounts, Theo must use
all of his legal powers to chase down the real thief.
Can Theo convince the police he's the victim of a
crime he did not commit?

THEODORE BOONE:
THE ABDUCTION

'HEY, LEEPER! WHERE'S APRIL FINNEMORE!?'

LEEPER OFFERED A NASTY GRIN AND YELLED
BACK, 'YOU'LL NEVER FIND HER.'

'IS SHE ALIVE?'

'YOU'LL NEVER FIND HER.'

THEODORE BOONE'S best friend April has
disappeared in the middle of the night. The only
suspect is an escaped convict, and he won't give
them any answers.

Thirteen-year-old Theo – the son of two lawyers –
knows the criminal justice system. Terrified that he'll
never see April again, he begins his own
investigation.

But as the days drag on with no new leads, Theo
starts to think the police are chasing the wrong
person. Can he hunt down the truth and find his
friend – or is it really too late?

THEODORE BOONE

'SAY, THEO. DO YOU THINK MR DUFFY IS GUILTY?'

'HE'S PRESUMED INNOCENT.'

'GOT THAT. BUT WHAT'S YOUR OPINION
AS TO HIS GUILT?'

'I THINK HE DID IT.'

THEODORE BOONE is thirteen and wants nothing
more than to swap homeroom for the courtroom; he
lives for big trials. Now the biggest murder case in
his city's history is set to begin.

In the packed court, a husband awaits trial for his
wife's murder. Is he a dangerous criminal or an
innocent victim?

The case takes a sinister twist when Theo uncovers a
surprise witness with his own problems to hide. But
Theodore is sworn to secrecy and time is running out.

Can Theo find a way to bring the killer to justice …
or will a guilty man get away with murder?